PROVOKED—A SCI-FI ALIEN WARRIOR ROMANCE

Raider Warlords of the Vandar #6

TANA STONE

Broadmoor Books

CHAPTER ONE

Vassim

I dragged the blade of my battle axe across my leather kilt, the slick blood darkening the garment but leaving the curved steel glinting in the light of the setting suns.

"It was a valiant battle, Raas." My *majak*, Taan, strode over from where he'd dispatched an imperial soldier, his opponent's helmeted head rolling across the dusty ground away from its uniformed body.

I surveyed the enemy bodies scattered across the ground, and beyond them, the gray silhouettes of the Zagrath ships hunched in front of the turquoise waters that the people of this planet called the shallows. The sunlight bounced off the surface of the water, sending a golden glow over everything and almost masking the horrors of the battle with its beauty.

"We honored Lokken," I said, invoking the Vandar god of old who blessed our battles.

My second in command tipped his head up to the sky where the enemy battleship lit up the sky as it exploded in a flash of white. "And saved the planet from being taken by the empire."

I growled, a swell of pride surging through me at the sight of the explosion, and the thought of thwarting our enemy's efforts to exert control over yet another less powerful planet. When I'd directed my Vandar horde to respond to a distress call sent out by Kimithion III, I'd been more curious about the Vandar raider who'd sent it, but now that we'd tasted enemy blood, I almost forgot about the exiled raider who'd piqued my curiosity.

I hooked my axe on my belt. "It has been a long time since we've taken down a Zagrath fleet."

"I have missed it," Taan confessed, although his voice held no condemnation.

I flicked my gaze to him, nodding. "I, as well."

We did not need to speak the rest, for we both knew it all too well. Our horde had been patrolling the far reaches of space and away from almost all imperial activity for so long that the Zagrath had become like a shadow enemy to us. Although we maintained a sort of loose order on the lawless hinterlands, the empire had abandoned the space long ago. Perhaps even before our horde was relegated to patrol it.

Cursed to patrol it, I thought, before forcing the traitorous words from my mind. It did not do any good to reopen old wounds, especially ones that were not old enough. I swallowed the sharp tang of bile and drew in a deep breath.

"There are no more imperial soldiers, Raas," said Taan, interrupting my thoughts, "and the fleet appears to be in tatters." My *majak* clicked his heels together. "What are your orders?"

I cut my gaze to the soldiers scattered like broken dolls across the ground. "Burn the bodies. I will speak with Corvak and the natives before we depart."

He clicked his heels once more in salute before spinning on his heel and striding toward the carnage, calling other raiders to help him with a sharp *"Vaes!"*

The battle had both fired my blood and stilled my rage, dousing a long-suppressed desire to strike a blow against the empire. Seeing the faceless Zagrath soldiers being piled up, helmets gleaming, reminded me that I was a Raas of the Vandar, even if I had not laid eyes on another warlord of my people since before I'd been named Raas.

I breathed in deeply as I walked away from the battlefield and toward the village we'd been fighting to protect, the salt in the air reminding me that the natives of the planet had evolved from the seas and still resembled aquatic creatures. The humans who shared the planet with the native Kimitherians did not share the green-blue scales and webbed hands and feet, but to me they were equally foreign. Smaller in stature than Vandar, humans did not have tails or marks across their chests, and their mating was not fated like ours.

But if the rumors were true, my fellow Raas' had claimed human females as mates, a phenomenon I found to be both startling and inexplicable. I could hardly believe that my fellow warriors had crossed paths with these creatures, much less taken them as mates. From the little I'd seen, the females were small and unskilled in battle. I failed to see the appeal.

When I reached my transport ship, I was pleased to see Corvak, the Vandar who'd sent out the initial distress call, approaching from the other direction. Dirt covered his bare chest, along with mating marks that were spreading across his shoulders and up his neck even as I watched.

"Raas Vassim." He bowed his head and clicked his heels once he reached me.

"Battle chief," I said, acknowledging the position he'd occupied before he'd been exiled from his horde. I knew his story, and although I understood why Raas Bron had punished him for questioning his authority, I also believed that Corvak's desire for the truth and lust for battle made him an ideal Vandar raider.

He looked over my shoulder to the pyre of imperial bodies being stacked high. "You were victorious."

"We showed no mercy to the imperial encroachers." I gazed upon at the sky that was now empty of Zagrath ships. "Your bounty hunter friends were just as merciless."

"Kimithion III owes both of you a great debt."

I inclined my head at him. "And you."

His cheeks colored. "I had a more personal reason to wish to save the planet."

I glanced at his mating marks. "Will this reason keep you here?"

He gave a definitive shake of his head. "I am destined to be in the skies, not on the ground."

I folded my arms over my chest. Even though our ancestors had been nomads who'd roamed the plains of our home world, their hordes traveling on the backs of beasts and living in yurts made of skins, I also felt more of a connection to space. It had been a millennium since we'd been forced off Vandar and into the skies, and although we maintained much of our traditions in our weapons, attire, and organization, few raiders longed to return to a life on land. "If you truly wish to leave, you are welcome to join my horde."

Corvak's eyes flashed with longing. "I am honored you would offer me a place in your horde, especially after I was—"

"Bron was the wrong Raas for you." I cut him off. "You need a leader who values breaking the rules."

His lips quirked, and I wondered how much he'd heard about me. It was no secret that whispers had reached the other sectors that I was *lunori*, the Vandar word for deranged. The Vandar had a reputation for being violent raiders who showed no mercy to their enemies. That was true of every horde. But it was said that I'd gone beyond that with my madness. That I tore my victims apart with my teeth, and that my horde feasted on the flesh of our kills. It was said that patrolling the hinterlands had made me lose my grip on reality and that I wandered my warbird raving and wailing. The rumors were only partially untrue.

"Your offer honors me, Raas Vassim." He lowered his eyes. "But my mate has agreed to leave the planet with me, and I have promised that I will not take her too far from her home. We will be joining the bounty hunters, who will remain near this sector."

I cocked an eyebrow at him. "Your mate is from Kimithion III?"

He raised his eyes to meet mine, obviously fighting the smile teasing his lips. "She is human. I have been training her as a warrior since I arrived."

Now I smiled, a rare occurrence that surprised even me. "A human female who is also a warrior? At least that explains her appeal."

He shifted from one foot to the other. "I was as surprised as you. I never intended to find my true mate on Kimithion III, and before meeting Sienna I would never have believed I could care for a human."

"You are sure, then?"

He clicked his heels and bowed his head once more. "I am grateful for the offer, Raas, but I promised my mate that we would stay closer to Kimithion III."

I grunted but nodded. "I do not understand the appeal of these human females, but I respect your mating marks. If you have made a promise, you should keep it. It is true we will be returning to the hinterlands once we leave this primitive place."

I glanced back at my raiders, who were preparing our transports for departure. As rewarding as it had been to battle the empire, I was more at home in the wild sector of space. It was the fate I deserved.

"The residents of Kimithion III extend their gratitude for your assistance, as do I," Corvak said. "We would not have defeated the empire without you and your raiders."

"That is true." I unfolded my arms and rested one hand on the hilt of my battle axe, drumming my fingers. "Destroying a Zagrath battleship was its own reward, as was cutting down the soldiers they sent to the surface. It has been too long since my warriors and I tasted imperial blood."

Corvak's gaze dropped to my chest and the blood that was no doubt splattered across it, but I ignored the flicker of fear that crossed his face. "If you ever tire of hunting bounties, you always have a place in my horde. Your lust for vengeance and talent for torture would be put to good use, battle chief."

"It would be an honor to serve you, Raas."

I spotted a human female walking purposefully toward us, her golden-brown hair spilling across her shoulders, and black marks peeking up from beneath the neckline of her shirt. "Once you have sated your lust for your mate, of course. There is no place for a female on a Vandar warbird roaming the hinterlands, even one who fights."

He twitched, and I suspected he could sense his mate approaching. "Yes, Raas."

I turned to board my ship, then swiveled back around. "One more thing, Corvak. The empire sent a lot of firepower to take a planet of caves and dirt. I suspect it does not have anything to do with their plentiful algae."

His face contorted. "It does not."

I raised a palm to silence him. "You do not need to tell me. It is better I do not know. That way, I do not have to deny anything." I twisted my hand to reveal a thin scar across the back of it. "I suspect it has something to do with my vanishing scar."

He opened his mouth, but I shook my head. I'd surmised the planet's secret, and my healing scar had only proved it. "Do not worry, battle chief. Their secret is safe with me. The last thing I would wish for is immortality or regeneration. Not when I chase death with such determination."

I left him speechless as I joined my warriors and the crates of gifts that the Kimitherians were insisting we take as expressions of their gratitude. The last thing Vandar raiders wanted was kelp jerky, but we also did not want to dishonor them.

"We take it all with gratitude," I told them, bowing to the natives standing off to the side who bobbed their scaly heads. Then I proceeded up the ramp and into the largest transport, the one I'd had specially outfitted for longer journeys.

Loading the crates would take some time, which meant we couldn't depart immediately. I huffed out a breath, scolding myself for being impatient, as I stalked to the private Raas chamber in the back. Why did I want off the planet so desperately? Especially now that I knew of its healing abilities?

But I knew the answer to my own question. I didn't deserve to be healed. Not as long as I was cursed with nightmares that made sleep impossible. The tales of the deranged Raas wandering his horde ship were not altogether false. I chased away sleep and the inevitable torture that came with it in any way I could, which often meant that I haunted the dark corridors of my warbird, nearly mad from lack of sleep.

The Raas chamber I stumbled into was dark and small, equipped with a thickly padded chair that looked much like a glossy, black egg. I sank into it and reclined, letting the exhaustion of the battle wash over me. As much as I fought it, my eyes fluttered shut.

Almost instantly, I was transported to the battle on Porvak. The char in the air burned my nostrils and made my mouth taste of ash. Steel clanged against steel as we battled the barbarian natives who'd drawn our horde into battle. But it was the scream of my Raas, Raas Oddon, that pulled my gaze away from my opponent. As soon as I heard him, I ran across the rocky terrain, leaping over bodies and dodging boulders. But as fast as I ran each time, I was never fast enough.

My heart raced as I bent over the Raas, a massive Porvakian blade sticking from his chest. Blood trickled from his mouth as he pulled me to him, begging me to pull it out. I flinched, shaking my head. But each time in my dreams, as in life, I did what he asked, jerking the blade from his chest. And each time, the blood spilled from him and over my hands, and the Raas I'd sworn to protect died in my arms.

I jerked awake, panting and drenched in sweat as the ship touched down with a jolt. We were already back on the horde ship? Even though my nightmares always left me weary, I must have been asleep for a while.

I staggered from the Raas chamber and the ship, the rattle of the metal ramp rousing me completely by the time I set foot onto the hangar bay floor.

"Are you ready to depart, Raas?" Taan asked, when he met me at the bottom of the ramp.

"Affirmative."

He conveyed my orders to the command deck, and the engines of the warbird rumbled as we accelerated. Before we could leave the hangar bay and proceed to the command deck, Taan grabbed my arm and nodded to the transport.

At the top of the ramp stood a human female with hair the color of spun gold. I stopped breathing as the seer's prophecy rang in my ears.

CHAPTER TWO

Juliette

This was all wrong. I was supposed to be on the bounty hunter ship. But one glance at the exposed iron beams and ebony walls told me that I'd made a huge mistake. Then I spotted the Vandar raiders standing at the bottom of the ramp.

What have you done, Juliette?

The pounding of my heart was almost deafening as the warrior in the center of the group stepped forward, his tail snapping behind him. Black studded leather sheathed his forearms, and a matching strap crossed his chest, spiked armor extending over one shoulder. Straight hair as black as ink fell down his back, and the dark slashes of his eyebrows pressed together.

Even though my mouth was dry, I managed to speak. "Who are you?"

He cocked his head slightly at me, his tail curving up behind his back and going still, only the tip quivering. "I am Raas Vassim of the Vandar, but many call me *Lunori* Raas, the Deranged Warlord."

I met his gaze, realizing that this Vandar was unlike anyone I'd ever seen before, including the only other Vandar I'd known, Corvak. This was a warlord, presumably the one who'd just saved my planet from the empire, and his eyes were those of a predator. He looked me up and down, making no effort to hide his bold appraisal. I might not have any experience with males, but even someone as sheltered as me knew what the flare of his pupils meant. Either he desired me, or he was about to kill me.

Before I could determine which was more likely, my knees buckled, and everything around me went black. I was only vaguely aware of strong arms catching me before I hit the floor.

"She's waking!" The voice sounded like it came from the end of a long tunnel.

I blinked a few times, the faces coming into sharper focus. I was lying on the floor, but my head was elevated slightly. "Where am I?"

"You are full of questions." The deep rumble of his voice reverberated in my own body, and I realized that it was Raas who held my head on his lap. The Vandar warlord who'd looked at me like I was lunch.

I attempted to sit up, but he held me down.

"You should not be so quick to move. You fainted."

My cheeks burned with embarrassment, although I didn't know why I should care what a bunch of Vandar raiders thought about me. It wasn't like they'd expect a human woman to be tough. Still, I couldn't help thinking of what my sister Sienna would say about me fainting. She'd never pass out at the sight of a bunch of Vandar. She'd probably cheer and ask them for an axe.

Sienna. I suddenly remembered why I'd stowed away on the ship I thought belonged to the bounty hunter crew. My older sister had left our planet with the Vandar raider she'd fallen for, and they'd both joined the bounty hunters who'd helped save Kimithion III.

I'd had the bright idea of joining her, but I'd had to stow away, since Sienna was still furious at me for betraying her to a guy who'd then taken her captive. It had been stupid of me, but I'd been terrified of her leaving me and thought that torching her relationship with Corvak would keep her on Kimithion III. Instead, I'd put my sister in danger, and given her even more reason to leave.

"My sister," I said, my voice cracking. "I was trying to find my sister."

The Vandar who were leaning over me exchanged confused looks.

"I can promise you that your sister is not on a Vandar horde," the Raas said. "At least, not this one."

I gave my head a small shake, which made it ache. "She was going with Corvak and the bounty hunters."

The Raas lifted an eyebrow. "You are the sister of Corvak's mate?"

Putting a hand to my temples, I nodded slowly. "I'm Juliette, her younger sister."

"You do not resemble her."

My cheeks heated again, as I remembered being teased for being plump, and Sienna fighting anyone who dared to call me fat. "She's always been the skinny one, and I've always been, well, not."

His brow furrowed. "I do not mean the shape of you." He brushed a strand of hair off my cheek. "Your hair is so much lighter than hers."

"Oh. I look more like our mother, I guess." My gaze went to his long, black hair that fell forward as he peered down at me, then to the dark marks on the exposed skin of his muscular chest. I'd never been so close to anyone who wore so little. I tried to push myself up again. "I can't stay here. I need to find my sister."

"You stowed away on a Vandar ship," the Raas said, making no attempt to stop me from sitting up this time.

"By mistake. It was a new moons night, so I couldn't see very well in the dark." Not that I could tell the difference between a bounty hunter ship and a Vandar one.

The Vandar raiders surrounding me shifted and muttered darkly. Clearly, that wasn't the right thing to say.

"Have you ever been on a spaceship before, human?" the Raas asked.

I moved off of him and twisted around so I faced him, pulling my dress around my legs and tucking my ankles behind me. "No."

"But you thought it would be a good idea to sneak aboard a ship without asking for permission to board?"

This wasn't going in the direction I'd hoped it would. No one was rushing to track down my sister's ship or rushing to send me back to my planet. I blew out an irritated breath. "I couldn't ask permission because I was afraid Sienna would say no."

"You believed your sister would reject your request?" another Vandar asked, this one without the chest straps or shoulder armor of the Raas, but with locks just as long and dark.

I looked away. "She was angry with me, but I couldn't let her leave without apologizing. That's why I snuck onto your ship. I was trying to find my sister so I could make amends. So can you please help me find her?"

The Raas stood, towering over me as he cut a quick glance to the other Vandar who'd addressed me. "The bounty hunter ship is far from here, is that not right, Taan?"

The Vandar called Taan gave a sharp nod. "They left before we did, Raas. We do not know their course."

My heart sank. Sienna was gone. I'd lost my chance to tell her how sorry I was, and how deeply I regretted betraying her. I stood, so I wouldn't have to crane my neck to meet the Vandars' eyes. "Then you can return me to my planet."

The Raas crossed his arms over his chest and stared at me.

"Please?" I added.

He studied me for a few moments longer, and I squirmed under his scrutiny. I wasn't used to males noticing me, and I definitely wasn't used to them staring at me like this Raas did.

He pivoted to Taan. "How far are we from Kimithion III, *majak*?"

"We have been traveling at full impulse since we returned to the warbird. We should be nearly an astro unit away from the alien planet."

I looked from one warrior to the other. "What's an astro unit? What does that mean?"

"It means we are too far away to go back to Kimithion III." Raas Vassim leaned closer to me. "Which means I am not returning you to your planet."

I gaped at him as the words sunk in. "What do you mean you're not returning me?" I reached out and grabbed his arm. "You have to!"

A few of the raiders inhaled sharply and then the group went silent. Raas Vassim didn't react, apart from the muscle that quivered in his jaw. I dropped my hand and stepped back, feeling the first flash of real fear since I'd walked onto the ship.

"I do *not* have to return you to your planet, female," the Raas said, his voice low and silky, almost masking the deadly hum beneath it. "I am the Raas of this horde. I do not answer to anyone. And in case you haven't heard the rumors, I am called the Deranged Raas because I do not follow the rules of war. I do not do what others think I should do, and I do not bow to the demands of stowaways."

Terror coiled its cold fingers around my heart as I peered up into the pools of cold darkness that were his eyes. "I didn't mean to demand. I'm…I'm sorry. I just want to go home."

"You were running from home, were you not?"

I opened my mouth, then clamped it shut. I had been running as far from my home world as I could get, but I hadn't expected to end up *this* far.

The Raas lowered his head so that it was next to mine, dropping his voice to a purr that sizzled down my spine. "You might not have meant to stow away onto my ship, female, but you did. That makes you the property of the Vandar, and of me. I cannot return you to your planet, or the bounty hunters, because you belong to me. This horde ship is your home now."

I sucked in a breath as his tail curled around my waist, keeping me from staggering away from him.

He drew in a deep breath at my neck, as if smelling my skin, then his deep groan sent a jolt through me. "The only thing I have yet to figure out is exactly what I'm going to do with you."

CHAPTER THREE

Vassim

I stepped back from the female, steadying my breath and looking away from her stricken face. I jerked my head to Taan. "Take her to my quarters."

Taan inclined his head and snapped his heels together. "It is done, Raas."

"Wait!" The female dodged my *majak's* attempts to grab her, spinning from the grasp of my tail and out of reach of both of us. "You can't just take me captive."

Even though her efforts were futile, I did admire her tenacity. It was more than I'd expected when I'd first seen her and after she'd fainted.

"I am not taking you captive," I said. "I am holding an alien who stowed away on my ship. Normally stowaways on Vandar warbirds aren't retained. They're put out the nearest airlock."

She swayed on her feet, and I wondered if I'd have to catch her again. I wouldn't mind holding her once more. The human with gold hair and lots of curves intrigued me. Her skin smelled of sugar, and her eyes were the color of the Jugerian seas. Not to mention the fact that she might be the female in the prophecy.

My stomach tightened. I hadn't allowed myself to hope that the words the seer had spoken to me would ever be anything but a fantasy. They'd seemed so far-fetched that I hadn't even bothered to search for the thing she'd claimed would cure me of my cursed dreams.

A female with hair like the sun and a heart and body as pure as gold.

There had been scant few females with pale hair in the far reaches of space where we patrolled and even fewer that could be considered anything close to pure. I'd put the witch's words from my mind and accepted that I would never close my eyes without reliving the torture of my Raas' death again and again.

"So why aren't you putting me out an airlock?" the human asked, squaring her shoulders.

I made no secret of eyeing her curves. "You have more of value than most stowaways."

Even though her eyes were a cool blue, they flashed with challenge as she fisted her hands by her side. "I'm not going to be your whore, if that's what you're planning. I'd rather die first."

Her fire stoked heat in my own belly, but I only smiled at her. "I have no intention of forcing myself on you, female. Vandar raiders might pillage, but we do not rape. We do not need to. Females are eager to warm our beds, whether in pleasure houses or not."

That was true, although it had been a long time since I'd joined my raiders on one of our stops at the pleasure planets. It was part of my self-imposed penance. If I did not deem myself worthy of a female from a pleasure house, I would never be worthy of an innocent like this human. She did not know how safe she actually was from me.

Her tight fists relaxed, even as her cheeks flushed. "Is that a promise?"

I gritted my teeth. I was not used to having my word questioned. Then again, this female seemed to know little about the Vandar. "It is a promise. A Raas doesn't lie."

She didn't seem totally convinced, but she finally nodded. "Okay. I guess I have no choice but to trust you."

"That is correct." I stepped closer to her and wrapped my tail around her waist. "You have no choice, although I assure you that you will not be harmed. Consider yourself to be our guest."

Her lips parted slightly as she looked up at me. Her innocence was so foreign to me it was almost intoxicating. The slightest touch from me made her skin turn pink and the vein in the side of her neck throb. How would she react if I jerked her body to mine and crushed my lips to hers? My fingers tingled and my cock twitched as I imagined the feel of her soft curves pressed to my hard muscle.

I tore my gaze from her before my mind wandered any further and made my arousal evident to every warrior standing with me, as well as to the human.

"*Vaes*," Taan said to her, but did not reach for her.

She tilted her head at him. "*Vaes?*"

"It means 'come.' You did not learn Vandar from Corvak?" I asked.

"I didn't talk to him. That was all Sienna. I thought he was a terrifying barbarian." She slapped a hand over her mouth, her eyes widening in horror at the insult she'd just levied at the Vandar.

Before I could respond, Taan spoke. "I assure you we are not barbarians. Would barbarians travel in warbirds large enough for hundreds to live on board? Would those same warbirds be able to fly invisibly if we were barbarians?"

She shook her head, dropping her hand. "I didn't mean anything. It's just what everyone said when Corvak arrived on our planet. We'd never seen anyone as huge, or with as little clothing. And we'd never seen an axe before. Weapons were never allowed on Kimithion III." She glanced around the hangar bay. "But you're obviously more advanced than my planet, so I guess we're really the barbarians."

"Then you are the most attractive barbarian I've ever encountered," Taan said.

The female gave him a smile she hadn't given me, and jealousy stabbed at me. Taan had always been known for his skill at seducing females, regardless of their species. I'd seen him at work many times, but never with a female who captured my interest. Or one who could be the solution to my curse.

Instinctively, I growled low, the tip of my tail twitching.

Taan glanced at me with a tip of his head. "Would you like me to escort the female to your quarters, or would you prefer to do it, Raas?"

His calm voice reminded me that he was my loyal first officer, and would never betray me. Not only that, but seduction was second nature to Taan, a skill he employed to get females to do what he wished. It didn't mean he planned to claim her. He was merely charming her to make her easier to handle. His honeyed words had been the reason we'd gotten a warm welcome from the queen on Sobari, and a deep discount on our supplies from the female clerk at the last outpost we'd visited.

"You can escort her." I locked eyes with him for a moment. "Then join us on the command deck."

With a quick tap of his heels, he turned and guided the human away from me and out of the hangar bay. I watched her go, curious when she gave me a final glance over her shoulder before the door swished shut behind them.

Once Taan and the female were gone, I turned to the nearest officer. "Alert the command deck that we're changing course."

"Yes, Raas. Do you have a new destination for our navigator?"

"Qualynn," I said, not looking at the surprised expressions I knew would cross my raiders faces.

It had been a long time since the horde had visited the mystical planet of Qualynn, but I needed to speak to the witch again. I had to know if my stowaway was also the one female who could save me.

CHAPTER FOUR

Juliette

After the door to the Raas' private quarters slid shut behind me, I stood in place without moving. Part of me was rooted to the spot in fear after what had just happened, and part of me was startled by the large space in which the menacing warlord lived.

"What is this place?" I whispered to myself, the hush of my voice cutting through the quiet.

The walk through the Vandar warbird had been enough of a shock. After living in stone dwellings cut into beige stone all of my life, the dimly-lit ship that seemed to be all exposed iron and lurking shadows was something I'd never seen before. Trekking up the suspended walkways and open-weave corridors reminded me a little of the winding path up the rock face on Kimithion III, but that was where the similarities ended.

While my home planet had two suns that provided endless rays of light, the Vandar kept the labyrinth of their warbird dark, with only glowing blue-and-purple lights to provide any illumination. The core of the ship was open, so I'd been able to tip my head up and see the outlines of walkways and spiraling staircases crisscrossing overhead. Heavy boots and deep voices echoed off the metal as raiders moved around, adding to the throaty rumble of the engines.

I allowed myself to release a breath and the fists I'd been holding tightly by my side. The walk to the Raas' quarters might have clued me in that I wasn't on Kimithion III anymore, but it hadn't prepared me for the place where the Raas who'd referred to himself as *lunori,* or deranged, lived.

Like the rest of the Vandar ship, the room was bathed in darkness, the only light coming from a fireplace built into one glossy, ebony wall. The crackling flames sent gold light flickering across the expansive room, showing me flashes of weapons mounted on walls, and a single wall of curved glass that overlooked space. There was no bed that I could see, only black, cushioned pallets topped with a profusion of pillows and swaths of haphazardly tossed fur throws. Open books were scattered on the pallets, and pewter goblets rested on the floor next to them.

I eyed the setup. "I guess there's no maid on a Vandar warbird."

I fought the instinct to close the books and straighten the blankets. Not only did I not want to risk moving something and angering the Raas, *but I also wasn't* here to clean up after him. Not that I really knew why I was here.

I took tentative steps around the room, brushing my fingers over a board of tiny steel spikes hanging on the wall and a target with slender blades protruding from the pockmarked surface.

What kind of games did the Raas play in here? I shuddered, trying not to let my imagination run wild imagining Vandar entertainment. Although the Raas had promised not to force me to do anything, he hadn't convinced me that he wasn't a violent brute, and the collection of weapons strapped to the walls didn't change my mind.

"It's just a Vandar thing," I told myself, as I dared touch a metal orb covered in knobby bumps hanging from a bar.

For the briefest moment, I considered using the weapons on display against the Raas. He'd come in here eventually, and he'd never expect me to attack him with…I looked at a curved blade fastened to the wall, the shiny blade glinting in the firelight. I didn't even know what any of these ancient weapons were called. No way could I use them effectively against a battle-hardened, Vandar warrior. I'd never even thrown a punch.

I shivered as I remembered the way Raas Vassim moved, his tail twitching almost imperceptibly and his pupils so huge they'd swallowed up almost all of the brown iris. Nope. I didn't stand a chance against him, and I suspected he wouldn't appreciate me attempting to kill him.

Knowing that I was stuck on a ship with a warlord who lived and breathed battle to the point that weapons were his only room decor did not help quell my nerves. I cursed my stupidity. How had I gotten on the wrong ship? I should have known it was too small to be the bounty hunters' cruiser, but I'd doubted my instincts. Besides, what did I know about spaceships? Nothing. Which was why I'd ended up sneaking onto the wrong ship and getting caught by the Vandar.

"This never would have happened to Sienna."

My sister was too shrewd and clever to do something like this. My heart ached as I thought about my older sister, who was probably living blissfully on the bounty hunting ship with her new Vandar mate, with no clue that her idiot kid sister was in trouble.

Pausing at an arched doorway, I peeked my head inside. Before I saw the water, I smelled it. Although it didn't carry the scent of brine like the air near the shallows in my home world, there was no mistaking the moisture heavy in the air. I drew in a greedy breath as I stepped inside, the sweet perfume of the bubbling baths a welcome change from the armory on display in the bedroom.

I didn't know what I'd been expecting from a Vandar bathroom, but this wasn't it. Even though it was made from the same obsidian stone as the rest of the space, blue dots of light were embedded in the ceiling, creating the sensation of a twinkling canopy of stars overhead. Once my eyes had adjusted to the sapphire glow, my gaze was immediately drawn to the source of the water. A large, sunken, circular pool sat in the middle of the floor, with a small circle in the heart of it filled with ice-blue water, and triangular wedges shooting out from that. Each wedge featured a different color of water from crimson to orange to yellow to green.

I bent down and dipped my fingertips in the red water, the heat making me pull them out quickly before easing them back in and letting my flesh adjust to the temperature. Compared to that, the orange water was tepid and the yellow and green not heated at all. I couldn't reach the center circle, but I could tell without touching it that it was ice cold. Each water had its own scent, and the mingling aromas made my nose twitch.

Hiking my dress up, I kicked off my sandals, sat on the stone ledge of the crimson water, and lowered my legs slowly into the pool. The warmth caused a breathy moan to escape my lips, and

I closed my eyes as I leaned back and let the heat wash away my fears.

"This isn't so bad." I scissored my feet in the water. I didn't have heated baths like this at home, and I could definitely get used to it. As long as I avoided looking at the deadly weapons decorating the walls outside the bathroom.

I opened my eyes and scanned the smaller room. Maybe I could drag one of the pallets in here and never have to go back out to the weird, dungeon-like bedroom. Somehow, I didn't think the Raas would go for that. Not many would welcome a stranger living in their bathroom.

"Think, Juliette," I said to myself sharply. "How would Sienna get out of this situation?"

By kicking ass. Not an option for me. But maybe I could harness what I did have. Maybe I could sweet-talk Raas Vassim into letting me go. I swallowed hard as I imagined being in close proximity to the huge Vandar, and my heart thundered in my chest. His touch had been like fire scorching my skin and his tail…I shuddered as I remembered it around my waist.

"Baby steps," I whispered. "First, you have to talk to him without nearly passing out. Then you worry about the tail."

A swish outside the room made my spine stiffen. Someone had come inside. The pounding of my heart quickened. Someone who didn't need to knock.

CHAPTER FIVE

Vassim

"She is settled?" I asked, as Taan joined me on the command deck, standing shoulder to shoulder with me on the raised platform that overlooked the warriors at their dark consoles and the wide view screen.

"She is in your quarters, Raas." He stared straight ahead. "I don't know if I would say she is settled. She seems to be nervous about the arrangement."

"There is nowhere else for her. We have no brig or spare officer quarters, and I cannot put her in the warriors' bunks."

Taan snorted out a dark laugh. "She seems too timid to survive that."

"Agreed." I didn't voice the thought that she might not be as frightened as I'd first assumed. The fact remained that she was a human and a female, which meant she was significantly smaller and weaker than every Vandar on board. And she was from a peaceful planet with no access to weapons. The creature had probably never held a blade in her life. She would be smart to be scared.

"You are sure it is wise to keep a human female in your private quarters, Raas?" My *majak's* words were hushed. I knew he did not want the others to hear him questioning me, even if the concern was justified. "You have outfitted your sleeping chamber with many things we would usually keep from a prisoner."

"She is not a prisoner," I said a bit too quickly and too loudly. A few heads swiveled to us and then away again out of respect. "Not in that way. Besides, I doubt she would know how to use any of it."

"A blade is still a blade, even if it is only used for target practice to keep you awake."

I flinched at the reminder of all the tools I used to prevent myself from falling into a deep sleep and reliving the terror of my Raas' death. When I could no longer stand on the command deck without swaying from exhaustion, I would drink bitter tonics, read complicated battle tomes, throw knives, plunge myself into the ice bath, and even lean against the spikes on the walls until their prickly ends pierced my flesh. Anything to stay awake.

"I do not fear the female," I said, cutting a quick glance at Taan. "She might only be a human, but she is not a fool. I would be able to fend off any flimsy attack. Besides, if she tried to kill me, she must know she would be shown no mercy."

"But why keep her at all, Raas? Why not turn around and drop her back at her planet? You know it would take little time, and then we would be rid of the distraction. You yourself heard what happened when Corvak's horde took a human female aboard. Do you wish there to be dissent here, as well?"

A growl rumbled low in my throat, but I bit it back. "That was different. He suspected that female of being a danger. This female is clearly not."

"If you wish for female companionship, we can arrange to stop at a pleasure planet, Raas. It has been a considerable amount of time since you joined your crew and sampled the pleasures of a female."

"I did not take her for that." I tried to think of anything but the small, curvy female with the gold curls. She was so different from the sophisticated and sultry alien pleasurers that it was almost laughable to think of her as an alternative. Where they were practiced and confident, she was innocent and unsure. Remembering the quiver of her bottom lip and her wide blue eyes made my pulse race and my cock ache. I might not have taken her to claim her, but it was undeniable that she stoked something within me. Something I had not felt in a long time.

"Then why, Raas?" Taan shifted to face me. "If not to warm your bed, why go to the trouble?"

I inclined my head toward the wide stretch of glass that looked out into space. "We are not headed back to our sector. We are on a course to Qualynn."

"The mystical planet." That made the warrior let out a resigned sigh. "The prophecy. I suspected as much when the female walked down that ramp."

I nodded as his words trailed off. He was the only raider in my horde who knew why I wandered the ship at night and often looked deranged. He was also the only one who knew of the witch's prophecy, although he'd never put much store in her claims that my affliction was a curse.

Taan's brow furrowed, as he clearly thought back to what I'd told him, perhaps resurrecting memories he'd long discarded. "You believe this female is the one the witch meant?"

The curl of his lip told me all I needed to know about his opinion of the alien seer. "She is the first one we have encountered who fits the description."

Taan did not look convinced. "Is it not possible, Raas, that the witch described a female we would not likely encounter easily? When do Vandar raiders, who patrol the lawless edges of the known galaxy, come across females who are pure of mind and body? Or have hair of gold? Have you never considered she might have been sending you on a fruitless chase that would only increase your madness?"

"Of course I have!" My booming voice made my *majak* flinch and more heads turn toward us. But Vandar warriors were known for raised voices and violent outbursts, so it was not wholly unusual. When my raiders returned their attention to their beeping consoles, I cleared my throat. "I am not so easily taken in as you might believe, *majak*. I have not been searching for the female of the prophecy. I'd actually put it from my mind and relegated myself to living with the nightly torment, but then *she* appeared."

"How could a female so different from us be the one who helps you?" Taan frowned. "It doesn't make sense."

I shrugged and faced the view screen, squaring my shoulders. "The seer will tell me."

"You intend to take the human with you to see her?"

"It's the only way she can tell me if I've found the female from her prophecy." I didn't glance over at my *majak*, even though I could feel his gaze on me.

The mystical planet of Qualynn was not for the faint of heart, and I knew Taan was doubting my plan to take the innocent human with me. Not only was the alien seer located within the wildest pleasure house on a planet that was known for scorning rules or propriety, but we would have to cross through a swamp of illusions to reach it. Many had been known to disappear within the swamp's hallucinations and never emerge.

"If she is not the female from the vision?" Taan asked, pivoting back to face forward.

"We return to Kimithion III and drop her off. Trust me when I say I have no desire to keep a female in our horde if she serves no purpose."

Taan clasped his hands behind him and rocked back on his heels. "And if the witch says that she's indeed the answer to your torment?"

I cut my gaze to him. "Then she stays with me until I no longer wake in a cold sweat, feeling more exhausted than when I closed my eyes. She stays with me until I am no longer mad with guilt."

"Raas—"

I waved a hand to cut him off. "I know what you are going to say, my friend, but our Raas died on my watch. I was *majak*, and I was tasked with having his back, as you have mine. I failed in that duty, and nothing you can say will make me believe otherwise."

"The Porvakians overwhelmed our forces," Taan hissed, his voice matching the intensity of mine. "We never should have gone in the way we did. The Raas made a bad call."

I gave a sharp shake of my head, attempting to keep the memories that dogged my sleep from invading my waking hours. But still, flashes of the battle rushed at me—my boots slipping in the blood of my fellow raiders, their screams as the aliens' acidic flesh burned theirs, the coppery scent filling the air and making my stomach churn. "We are Vandar. We should have been victorious."

My first officer grunted, his response barely a whisper. "But we are not invincible."

We both glanced at the open console where my battle chief once stood. He'd also fallen at the battle with the Porvakians, and I had yet to appoint a replacement. At least his death had not been on me, but it haunted me in a different way. We'd been the two top officers to the Raas, fighting side by side, and I could not bring myself to put another in his place. Not yet.

I gripped the iron railing in front of us, weariness sinking into my bones and making my vision hazy. I was living proof that the Vandar were not impervious to pain or defeat—and I despised myself for it.

CHAPTER SIX

Juliette

I jumped up from the side of the pool, water streaming down my legs and puddling around my feet. I glanced around but saw no towels or anything I could use to dry myself. At least my dress wasn't wet, except for the hem. Holding my arms out for balance as I padded barefoot across the slippery floor, I held my breath and peeked from the arched doorway.

I'd expected to see the imposing Raas storming into his quarters, but it wasn't him. It wasn't a Vandar warrior at all. I squinted through the dim light from the fire as a small alien placed domed plates on a low table next to one of the pallets on the floor.

"Who are you?" I asked, too curious to let the creature leave without knowing.

He yelped as he spun around, a hand pressed to his heart. "Don't scare me like that!"

"Sorry." I walked closer to the alien, who couldn't have been more than a boy. But like I'd first thought, he wasn't a Vandar boy. "I didn't mean to startle you."

The alien with brown, nubby horns poking through a mass of dirty blond curls gave me a tentative smile. "It's okay. I shouldn't have been so surprised. I heard you'd been taken to the Raas' quarters. I guess I forgot for a moment." His gaze went to the bottom of my dress, dripping water on the floor. "You know there are some clothes you could wear in the bottom of that." He pointed to a series of doors and drawers inset in the black wall nearest the bathing area then made a face at my long dress. "That doesn't look practical."

I ignored his comment about my dress. It didn't make sense on a spaceship, but it had been practical on my planet. Instead, I eyed him back. "You aren't Vandar." Not only did he have horns, but he also wasn't wearing the battle kilt of the Vandar. Instead, he had on brown pants that reached slightly below his knees and a loose, cream-colored tunic. He did, however, like the Vandar, have a tail.

"Nope." He pulled his tail up into one hand and fiddled with the furry tip nervously. "I'm Neebix."

I hadn't heard of the Neebix, but I nodded as if I had. It was embarrassing to admit I hadn't heard of many other species aside from the Vandar and the Kimitherians who were natives of my home world. Since my planet went to great lengths to keep us isolated, there was virtually no contact with other species. Thinking or talking about the universe beyond our small planet had never even been encouraged, and my lack of awareness of other aliens made my face burn.

"Is it customary for Neebix to be on Vandar ships?" I asked.

He grinned widely and shook his head. "I think I'm the only one. You can't just up and join a Vandar horde if you're not born into it."

I held his gaze for a moment, hoping that would prod him into explaining more. When he didn't, I asked, "So how did you manage to get on? I'm guessing you weren't a stowaway, as well?"

He giggled then glanced around and twirled the fur on his tail faster. "I don't think anyone's dared to sneak onto a Vandar warbird before." He looked at me with a mixture of deference and suspicion. "Or wanted to."

I didn't explain that I hadn't wanted to stow away on a Vandar warbird. Saying I'd gotten on the wrong ship would not impress anyone, although I was sure it wouldn't stay a secret forever. "Okay, so you didn't sneak on."

He lowered his gaze to the floor. "I was taken from a pleasure house on Terrentela Prime. Raas Vassim saw me there and saved me."

I swallowed down a lump in my throat, sizing up the boy as being no more than ten human rotations. "You mean you were working there?"

He shifted from one foot to the other, not meeting my eyes. "I hadn't started. There was an auction for my..." he hesitated, "first time, but the Vandar arrived and Raas Vassim bought me outright."

Outrage replaced my discomfort. "He bought you?"

The boy's face snapped up. "To get me out of there. He told me I could be one of the apprentices on his horde ship, and I'd never have to do anything like that."

"Oh." I was taken aback by how quickly he'd sprung to the Raas' defense. "So you like working here? As an apprentice?"

The smile returned to his face. "Oh, yes. I might be the only apprentice who isn't a Vandar, but they don't treat me any differently. Raas Vassim won't allow it. When I get to the age of maturity, I can choose to become a raider in his horde, or I can return to my home world. It's up to me."

"Why don't you want to go back home now?"

He shrugged one shoulder. "I don't have any family left, so I wouldn't have anywhere to live, or any way to take care of myself. Once I'm trained up, Raas Vassim says I'll be man enough to make my own way in the world, or fight by his side." He puffed out his small chest.

If the Raas was so willing to give this child a choice, why was he holding me? He'd actually purchased this boy, yet he had no problem giving him the option to stay or go.

"What's your name?" I asked, sensing that the boy was comfortable talking with me.

"Baru."

"So, Baru." I lifted the dome off one of the plates he'd arranged on the low table and inhaled the savory aroma wafting up. "You'd say the Raas is a fair warlord?"

More head bobbing. "The fairest. As long as you are not his enemy, he will treat you well."

"Then why do you think he's refused to return me to my planet? Do I look like an enemy of the Vandar to you?"

The boy's face flushed, and he gave me a cursory once-over. "No, but the Zagrath look very much like humans."

"I'm not Zagrath. I'm a human from the planet Kimithion III. Your horde was just on my planet, fighting off the empire."

His gaze darted around the room. "There must be a reason the Raas won't take you back there. Maybe it's dangerous."

"Or maybe he likes holding women against their will," I muttered under my breath, replacing the dome and straightening.

Baru shook his head so hard his curls flopped around his forehead. "The Raas is not like that. He has never brought a female on board. Not since…" His words trailed off, but he continued quickly. "He doesn't even go down to the pleasure planets with the rest of the crew anymore."

I threw my arms open wide. "Then why won't he take me home?"

The horns tucked amid Baru's curly hair were flushed almost as pink as his face. "Maybe he thought you could help."

"Help what? I don't know anything about battle or ships or, well, much of anything. I promise you I don't have any skills that would help a Vandar Raas."

The boy huffed out a breath. "He doesn't need help with any of that kind of thing, but maybe he thought you could help rid him of his madness. You look kinder than most aliens we encounter."

"Madness? Is that why he calls himself lumori?"

"*Lunori*," Baru corrected. "And he's not the one who calls himself the Deranged Raas. It's everyone who sees him roaming the ship and talking to himself."

Just great. I was supposed to share a room with a warlord of the Vandar who was so crazy he talked to himself?

"How could I help someone who's crazy?" I started pacing a small circle as I scraped a hand through my hair. "I don't know anything about that kind of thing. What if he gets violent?"

"The Raas saves his violence for battle. He has never lifted a finger against anyone in his horde."

I spun around to face the Neebix boy. "But I'm not a part of his horde."

"I would have to disagree with that," Raas Vassim said, as he stepped inside his quarters and locked his deadly gaze on me.

CHAPTER SEVEN

Vassim

I'd almost forgotten I'd requested food to be sent to the female until I saw Baru standing with her. His cheeks looked sunburned, and his horns were scarlet.

"Raas Vassim, I..." He attempted to click his heels together but missed and almost stumbled over his own feet.

"Thank you for taking good care of our guest," I said. "You are free to go."

He almost tripped as he backed from my quarters, finally turning and bolting away with his tail in his hands.

"Do you terrify everyone?" The female's voice wasn't as shaky as it had been in the hangar bay.

"Baru was not terrified." I unhooked my shoulder armor and draped it over the stand next to the door. "The boy knows me well."

She made a noise in her throat that told me she didn't completely agree. I ignored it and continued to disrobe, pulling off the studded leather sheathing my forearms and tugging my feet out of my boots.

"What do you think you're doing?"

I glanced over and noticed the water pooled around her feet and the trail leading from the bathing chamber. "I see you've found the baths."

She folded her arms over her chest and took a step away from me. "I only dipped my feet in."

"Well, I am going to dip my entire body in." I hooked my battle axe on the stand and then took off my wide belt. "I have not bathed since the battle on your planet, and I do not plan on going to Qualynn wearing the blood of my enemies."

"What's Qualynn?"

I paused with my hands on the waist of my battle kilt. "The planet onto which you will accompany me."

Her mouth dropped open slightly. "You're letting me go?"

"On Qualynn?" I almost scoffed at the thought. "I would not be so cruel."

The hopeful expression on her face faded. "If it's so horrible, why are we going at all? Why are you taking me to the surface?"

I clenched my jaw. "It's necessary."

"Maybe for you, but not for me. I may be your captive, but you can't force me to go with you to a dangerous planet."

The quaver in her voice was back, but instead of making me feel sympathy, it only made me more determined. I needed to take her to the seer so that I could know once and for all if this fragile creature had any chance of saving me.

I advanced on her so quickly that she didn't have time to back away, wrapping my tail around her waist as I loomed over her. "You will go with me because you're at my mercy, female. Do I have to remind you of what I could do to a stowaway?"

She arched her back as if trying to get as far away from me as possible without being able to step away. "No, you already made it very clear that I should be grateful you haven't killed me yet."

"And so you should be." My gaze drifted from her glistening eyes to her plump lips, which were slightly parted as she breathed in and out rapidly. The urge to taste her pulsed through me, hot and urgent, but I fought the weakness and stepped back, releasing my tail's grip on her. "But you should also know that I am not taking you into a battle zone. Qualynn is not a violent planet, and there should be no enemies there. At least, not in the traditional sense of the word."

She didn't respond, so I continued.

"It is known as a mystical planet, inhabited by magical creatures and ruled by illusions and spells. I would not leave you there because it would be difficult for someone as unseasoned as you to resist. You would probably be forever lost in the fantastical world where nothing is what it seems."

"Then why are we going? It doesn't sound like the type of place that would appeal to Vandar raiders."

"For one, it has an impressive series of pleasure houses with pleasurers who have unrivaled skills and tricks. For another, a seer lives in one of those houses. She is the one I'm taking you to see."

"A seer? As in, someone who divines the future?"

"And can warn you of peril or predict your victories." The alien seer, Ferria, had done both for me.

The female shook her head. "I don't want anyone looking into my future. That's playing God."

I growled, recalling that humans had a sad belief in a single deity. "There are many gods, and the witch can talk to them all, if I ask her."

"A witch?" Her voice trembled with fear. "I'm not letting you take me to a witch. How do I know you're not selling me to her? Maybe she needs a virgin for her spells."

As soon as the words had rushed from her mouth, she looked stricken, and her cheeks became mottled with patches of pink. I cocked my head at her. I'd been almost certain of her purity, but hearing her confirm it made my pulse quicken.

"You overestimate Ferria's desire for human females." I closed the distance between us and cupped her chin in my hand, tilting it up so that she was forced to meet my eyes. "Although my own seems to be growing."

Her chin shook as she stared up at me, but her fear did nothing to douse my desire. In fact, feeling her body tremble made me want to dominate her even more. I dropped her chin and loosened my battle kilt so that it hit the floor with a thwack. Her eyes widened as she realized that I was completely naked, but she didn't pull her gaze away from mine.

"You will go with me to visit the seer." I returned my hand to her jaw, running my thumb across the soft skin of her cheek. "If you're lucky, she will tell me that you're not the female I need, and I'll let you go."

She drew in an uneven breath. "And if I'm not lucky?"

I dragged my thumb across her bottom lip. "Then you will remain here with me for as long as I command you to."

Then I stepped away from her and over the pile of my discarded kilt, turning and walking toward the bathing chamber. Only when I'd plunged myself fully into the icy pool in the center did the storm of desire begin to fade.

Tvek. The last thing I needed or wanted was to fall under the spell of a human, especially if she was not the one who could cure me.

CHAPTER EIGHT

Juliette

I tugged the heavy cloak around my shoulders as the chill from the purple fog swirled around my ankles. I'd been reluctant to take the heavy, fur-lined garment when the Raas had offered it to me on the transport, but now I was grateful.

I stole a furtive glance at the warlord standing next to me on the flat-bottomed boat as we skimmed through the strange marsh. Even though the planet's surface was cold and shrouded in damp fog, he wore only his battle kilt. His broad chest was covered by the thick strap of his leather shoulder armor and the dark swirling marks that were common on all the Vandar raiders, but that was it. Of course, that was more than he'd been wearing when he'd stomped off to his bath.

Despite the cold, my face burned as I thought back to watching the naked Raas walk away from me. I'd never seen a male undressed before, unless you counted my drunk father staggering from the bathroom in his underwear, which I didn't. But the Vandar didn't wear anything under their kilts, so when Raas Vassim had dropped his on the floor in front of me, he'd been completely bare-assed.

My pulse fluttered as a mental image of that ass filled my mind, and I kept my eyes locked straight ahead. What caused my heart to race even faster was the memory of what had been swinging between his legs as he'd taken long strides away from me. Even from behind, it had been hard to miss.

It made sense that the huge Vandar raiders would be huge everywhere, but I'd never been confronted with the reality of just how huge before. Although the thought of it made my mouth go dry, a faint flutter of curiosity and desire awoke inside me.

I immediately shook my head. *Don't be foolish, Juliette. The Raas of a Vandar horde doesn't desire you. Not when he could have any female he wanted.*

Raas Vassim shifted next to me, glancing down when I shook my head. "Are you unwell?"

I darted a lightning-quick glance to him and then away. "I'm fine."

He grunted and turned his attention back to the path our boat was cutting through the fog, steered by a slender, green-skinned alien using a pair of poles he maneuvered expertly in the soupy marsh.

See? He's not interested in you that way, no matter what he might have said. He only wants to see if you can break some crazy spell.

That thought should have been comforting, but it only made the backs of my eyes sting. I might not want to be forced to be the bed mate of a terrifying Vandar warrior, but I hated the thought that he'd probably never be attracted to someone like me. My sister might have always insisted that I was the pretty one, but that didn't change the fact that I was curvier than all the other girls on my planet. I'd tried to convince myself that I didn't care when boys had called me chubby, but I'd hated it. My only comfort had been in my baking—and sampling my own creations—which hadn't done anything to solve the problem.

Even standing next to Raas Vassim made me want to hide myself. The alien was all muscle; his chest and arms looked like they'd been carved from granite, and his stomach was a ripple of hard bumps. How was that even possible? Had he never eaten a roll in his life? The prospect of a breadless existence made me shudder.

"You are cold?"

The deep burr of his voice snapped me from my mental meanderings. I peered up at him, realizing that I'd actually shuddered thinking about a life with no bread. I almost laughed. "No. The cloak is warm enough. Thank you."

He frowned, a line appearing between his eyes. "You do not need to be afraid. Qualynn might appear strange, but it is not dangerous, as long as you stay by my side."

He didn't need to tell me twice. Since the moment we'd stepped off the transport ship and the lilac mist had stretched out curling tendrils to wrap invisibly around my legs, I'd been determined to stick to the Raas like glue.

Growing up on Kimithion III had kept me sheltered, but I'd never even imagined there could be a planet like Qualynn. Although we were moving through a thick marsh, in the distance I spotted the faint outline of floating islands suspended in the fog. If I tipped my head all the way back, there was an upside-down version of boats gliding through the marsh above us.

"It is an illusion," Raas Vassim said, tracking my gaze. "It only appears that they are upside down."

I shifted closer to him. "They aren't real?"

"No, they're real, but it is we who are upside down."

My stomach did a strange somersault as I peered more closely at the water our boat pilot was steering us through. It wasn't water. It was dense fog that spiraled around the tips of his poles, creating lavender eddies that evaporated as quickly as they were formed. And beneath that were more levels of vessels being propelled through the air.

I squeezed my eyes shut, not wanting to think about what I'd seen or what I thought I'd seen. None of it made sense, and my head ached if I tried to separate reality from illusion. All I knew was that I desperately wanted to get back on the Vandar warbird, and back to the solidness of a place that was not controlled by mystical powers.

A large warm hand closed over mine. "We're here."

I reluctantly opened my eyes as the alien steering our boat tied it to a post protruding from a floating island. The island was made from what appeared to be rock and soil, with a large, conical base extending below the surface of the fog, with iridescent roots poking out from the dirt and sparkling granules sifting down each time the island shifted.

The island itself wasn't as awe-inducing as what was on top. Plush moss the color of the turquoise shallows back home covered the ground, and a curious building perched on top of that, the ivory-stone parapets and turrets glistening through the pale-purple mist. Stories were stacked on stories, with outer staircases curling around towers, and spires reaching into the sky.

"What is this place?" I asked, a chill washing over me.

The Raas stepped onto the island and pulled me with him, nodding at the alien who'd steered our boat. "It's one of the pleasure houses. It's where Ferria lives."

"She's a pleasurer and a witch?"

"More like a madam and a witch." He wrapped an arm around me and hurried me forward toward the door, which had a small window at the top. Rapping sharply twice, he stepped back and waited.

Despite my nervousness, I was also curious to see what the house was like on the inside. I'd never seen an actual pleasurer, and my imagination ran wild with possibilities. Whatever I'd been envisioning, it hadn't been the face that appeared in the high window.

Gnarled and heavily lined, the face of a male alien scowled down at us. His nose resembled a sea cucumber that had been left out in the sun too long, and was the same sickly green color. "State your business."

"Raas Vassim of the Vandar is here to see Ferria for a consult."

The alien's beady eyes raked across the Raas, and then me. He snorted once, and disappeared from the window.

"Who—?" I began to ask, but was silenced by the scraping of the door opening. I was struck further speechless when I saw that the creature who'd appraised us at the high window only reached my knees. He was dressed in layers of colorful clothes and translucent, papery wings were tucked behind his back, the tips dragging the floor as he waved us forward.

Raas Vassim didn't release my hand as we followed the alien through a circular foyer. The ceiling was high and domed, with light streaming in from skylights, which I found odd, since from the outside the castle appeared to have no such roof. I'd expected to see lithe and scantily-clad females cavorting around, but there were none, and the only sound echoing through the stone foyer was a faint melody being played on a stringed instrument.

"Remember," the Raas leaned down and whispered to me. "Most of what you see won't be real."

I gripped his hand tighter as we passed through a curtained doorway, and into a room that was heavily perfumed and lit only with flickering candles. "Is that creature real?"

"In a manner of speaking, yes."

Before I could ask the Raas why he refused to give me a straight answer, the small male who hobbled along in front of us unfurled his wings, wrapping them around his body. The wings glowed as he appeared to grow before our eyes, and when he unwound them from himself, he was no longer a hunched creature. As a matter of fact, he was no longer a male at all. He'd transformed into a beautiful female with long, jet-black hair.

Raas Vassim gave her a small bow. "It is good to see you again, Ferria."

CHAPTER NINE

Vassim

It had been many rotations since I'd seen the seer, and even more since I'd seen her take the form of a Bederian winged troll. She blinked her luminous, green eyes at me, motioning for me to take a seat on the tufted red bench across the table from her.

"I would say you are looking well, Raas, but I would be lying." She steepled her fingers and looked over them at me, her gaze shrewd. "You have found no respite from your torment."

Even though she didn't ask it as a question, I answered. "No. My only escape is avoiding sleep."

She nodded. "Which is slowly driving you mad."

I opened my mouth to protest, but she flicked a finger at me. "Even here, the rumors of the *Lunori* Raas reach my ears. But I wonder if you are as deranged as they claim?"

I bristled at the boldness of her statements. I'd grown used to the whispers, but there were few who would dare question the sanity of a Raas to his face. Ferria was different. Her power humbled even me.

"There is still nothing you can do for me?" I asked. "No spell that can take away the nightmares?"

She leaned back and loosed a sigh. "As I have told you before, the curse that has been placed on you is not one that can be unraveled by a mere spell."

I growled in frustration. I had heard this claim from her lips many times, and each time it provoked an impatient rage. How had I become the first Vandar raider to be cursed during a battle?

"You might not have known the alien you slayed in battle was a powerful warlock," she said, as if reading my mind, which it was entirely possible she'd done, "but it's clear he managed to cast a curse on you with his dying breath."

I thought back to the alien I'd dispatched before hearing the cry of my Raas. He'd been lying on the ground, blood and unintelligible words burbling up through his mouth. Words that had been a curse he'd cast on me that forced me to relive the battle and my Raas' death—complete with the smells and sounds and pain—every time I attempted to sleep. If I could go back in time, would I have spared him? No, I thought, balling my hands into fists. I would have killed him quicker.

"But we aren't here to talk about why you were cursed, are we?" Ferria's gaze slid to the human. "You've come to me to ask me a question."

I glanced at Juliette, and my pulse quickened. Even in the candlelit room, her gold curls created a halo around her head, making her appear almost as otherworldly as the alien shifter witch. In this world, a being as innocent as her was as foreign as any magic.

I hadn't released her hand, and now that I wasn't focused on Ferria and my own bad recollections, I felt it trembling in mine. The human female who'd never set foot off her backwards planet was clearly petrified of the seer and the strange pleasure house. As much as I wished her to be the solution to my curse, a part of me thought it impossible that such a fragile, timid human could help me.

It was common knowledge that humans were smaller and weaker than Vandar, although like us, they were a species who'd left their home world millennia ago. Scattered throughout the galaxy, they were not known for exceptional battle skills or technological advances. How could one of them be the answer to anything?

A low rumble escaped my lips as I thought about the human female who'd snuck onto my ship. She might be slight and scared, but I could also not deny my desire to claim her. Perhaps it was because she was so unlike any females I'd encountered before that she stoked my need and fired my instinct to possess.

"Ask me." Ferria stared only at me and spoke now in my native Vandar tongue.

"*Hoon vak denini?*" I replied in Vandar. *Is she the one?*

The seer cut her gaze to Juliette again, narrowing her eyes. The human sucked in a breath, as if she was attempting to snatch it away from Ferria. Then Ferria reached out a hand and touched her cheek, a spark flashing between the two females' flesh.

The seer's lips curled into a smile. "How did a Raas of the Vandar manage to find such an unspoiled female?"

"She came to me."

Her arched eyebrows quirked. "Even better."

"So? I asked, hearing the snap in my voice. "Is she the one you foretold?"

Ferria gave me a curt nod, and relief coursed through me. I released Juliette's hand and scraped my fingers through my hair. "After all this time, it was a human."

"Yes." Ferria drummed her fingers together. "It's an unexpected turn of events."

I straightened, feeling a surge of power I hadn't experienced in a long time. "How long until I can expect the cure to break?"

Ferria smiled at me again, but this one was not kind. "Did you really think it would be that easy, Raas? That you would find the female from the prophecy and the curse would be gone?"

Her mocking tone made my hopeful heart grow cold and my anger flare. "You are playing with me, witch."

She made a soft *tsk*-ing noise in the back of her throat as she shook her head. "The only drawback to you big, gorgeous Vandar is your nasty tempers. I never told you that finding the female was the way to break the curse, only that you needed to find her in order to break it."

I tempered my anger, drawing in a breath to steady myself. "So what now?" I avoided looking at Juliette, whose head was toggling back and forth between us as we spoke in a language she didn't understand. "Do not tell me I need to claim her by force. I have given her my word I will not."

Ferria pressed a hand to her chest. "You wound me, Vassim. As if I would ever require a forced mating."

I made an effort not to scoff out loud. I knew exactly what type of pleasure house she ran and the spells she put on her pleasurers and visitors alike to eliminate their inhibitions. I'd been the recipient of them before, although I had been willing. All were not, and her protestations of innocence were laughable.

"Then what?" I said, between gritted teeth.

She stood and moved around the small room, her colorful skirts swirling as she pulled objects from shelves. A glass bowl appeared in the center of the table, making Juliette jump. As Ferria passed behind us, she snatched a single hair from Juliette's head without a word, provoking a yelp from the human. I took Juliette's hand again to calm her and found it like ice.

Ferria sat and added the hair to the bowl along with a violet powder and a clear liquid that poured from the silver bottle like syrup. She waved her hands over the concoction, and pink smoke rose from it, swirling into several shapes before tightening into a spiral and vanishing.

Ferria giggled as if she were a child, smiling up at both of us. "Quite the opposite, my dears."

"What's going on?" Juliette asked, jerking her hand from mine. "I agreed to come here because you said the witch might tell you to let me go. But you've both been talking in some strange language, and now she's made some sort of potion with my hair. For all I know, this could all be some show put on for my benefit, and it never had anything to do with you releasing me."

When she'd finished her rant, she glared at both is us.

"Not as helpless or as simple as she looks," Ferria said in Vandar, her voice tinged with admiration. Then she spoke in the universal tongue to Juliette. "I'm afraid I cannot tell Raas Vassim to release you, human. Not if he wishes to break his curse."

"What?" Juliette gasped.

Ferria ignored her and focused her gaze on me, switching back to Vandar. "To break the curse for good, you must take the female as your mate."

"But I already told you—"

"Not by force, Vandar." She rolled her eyes and muttered under her breath, "It's always force with these raiders." She locked eyes with me again. "She must come to you willingly before the alignment of the two moons of Vandar, and she must take your marks."

I sank down on the bench, her words like a punch to my gut. If I had to rely on Juliette taking my mating marks in order to break the curse, I might as well fly her back to her home world now. I wasn't worthy of any female's devotion, much less one who was as pure as this one. Even if she was strong enough to be a Vandar's mate.

I peered over at the small creature, her blue eyes wide and her plump lips quivering. Which she wasn't.

CHAPTER TEN

Juliette

The Raas didn't speak as we left the witch and walked back through the pleasure house. Though he hadn't taken my hand again, he did steer me forward by resting one hand lightly on my back.

I glanced over my shoulder at the seer, who hadn't stood from her chair when Vassim had jerked to standing. But when I returned my gaze for a final glimpse of the raven-haired female, she was gone, replaced by a fluttering insect with blue wings.

Shaking my head at this sight, I continued forward and back into the stone foyer. The Raas didn't pause in his long, purposeful strides, his kilt slapping his thighs, but I hesitated when I saw how the quiet space had changed since we'd been inside the room with Ferria.

It was no longer empty and nearly silent. The hall now buzzed with the chatter of voices, as females hung out of windows that hadn't been there earlier and leaned their ample bosoms over balconies that seemed to have appeared out of thin air.

"Where did—?"

"Do you believe in magic now?" the Raas asked in a gruff voice, tugging the door open and propelling us both through it.

Luckily, the outside of the floating island looked much the same, and the boat we'd arrived on was bobbing beside it, as if in a body of water. Raas Vassim handed me to the alien in the boat and leapt in beside me.

"*Duggari*," he growled. Then, when the alien gave him a blank look, he added. "Let's go."

We left the island and floated away, the gleaming castle fading quickly into the purple haze of fog. I had so many questions about the planet and the witch that I didn't know where to begin. But most of all, I had questions about what Ferria had said to me.

"Why can't you release me?" I asked the Raas, twisting to look up at him. "What curse was she talking about?"

He remained silent, pressing his lips together as the boat skimmed along through the mist.

"I thought you said the witch would tell you to let me go."

Finally, he met my eyes. "I said she might say that. It was what I was hoping."

That surprised me. "You were hoping she'd tell you to let me go? What happened to you keeping me because I stowed away on your ship?"

His expression was dark. "You are not meant for life on a Vandar warbird. I see that now."

Even though I agreed with him, I was annoyed that he'd said it. "You think I'm too sheltered and naïve to survive on your big, scary warship, is that it?"

He tilted his head at me. "Something like that."

"You know what?" I turned away from him and crossed my arms over my chest. "You don't know me as well as you think you do. If I'm so helpless, how did I manage to sneak onto your transport? I got past whatever guards or security you had, didn't I? Everyone always assumes I'm too scared to take a risk, and that Sienna is the one to be daring, but I can be brave, too. I just haven't had many chances before."

He made a sound that sounded a bit like a strangled laugh. "You're right. I don't know you. Maybe you are more courageous than others give you credit for. You did make it out of Ferria's without gaping too much. But you do not know me."

"I know you think you're cursed." I swiveled back to face him. "And that you need me to break it."

Another low grunt, but at least it was less hostile than the ones he'd emitted earlier. The boat touched onto another floating island, this one holding the landing pad and the Vandar transport ship. A pair of raiders stood on either side of the ramp with their hands on the hilts of their battle axes and their shoulders back.

"Ready to depart, Raas?" one of them asked as Raas Vassim helped me off the boat and slipped a gray velvet pouch into the boatman's hand.

"It is done," the Raas said, leading me up the ramp and onto the space vessel. He grabbed an overhead bar, curling an arm around my waist and his tail around my legs as the engine engaged, and the ship rocked back and forth as it pulled away from the surface.

Even though I tried to keep myself steady, I couldn't help leaning against his bare chest, my cheek touching the hard muscle. I put my hands on his stomach to brace myself, and he inhaled sharply. I wanted to move away, but the surging ship made it hard for me to keep my balance without him for support. What I didn't want to admit was that I liked the feel of his skin under my fingertips, and the heat from his body pulsing into mine.

"So are you letting me go, or not?" I asked, keeping my voice low.

Despite the rumble of the ship and the beeping of the computer, I sensed every Vandar on board tense.

"I am not," he said after a beat.

I pulled away from him, instantly missing the warmth of his skin on mine. "But I thought I wasn't Vandar material, that I couldn't hack it on your warbird."

He shrugged one shoulder. "You convinced me otherwise."

Just great. The one time I try to convince someone I'm tougher than I look, and they believe me.

"So I'm supposed to live the rest of my life on your ship?" The thought was incomprehensible. I'd never see my sister or my home again. And even though I'd been willing to run away, the thought of spending the rest of my life on a cold, dark horde ship filled me with dread.

"No. Only until the two moons of Vandar align."

"Do you make this little sense in your native language?" I asked. "That is what you and the witch were speaking, right? And by the way, that was pretty uncool. You could have been talking about me behind my back, and I wouldn't have known it."

"We were not talking about you. Not directly."

I huffed out a breath. "You know, I'm pretty sure it's women who're supposed to be the mysterious ones."

"My apologies, human. When the two moons of Vandar next align, I will return you to your planet."

"Really?" I couldn't resist smiling at him, but then I stopped and scowled. "Wait a second. You aren't going to tell me that the Vandar moons only align once every millennium, are you?"

The edges of his lips twitched. "No. They will align in a little less than two of your moon cycles."

I did a quick mental calculation. "That's not so long." I eyed him with suspicion. "What's the catch?"

"You will remain in my quarters and share my bed."

I gulped. "Does that mean…?"

"My promise remains. I will not force you to do anything. I will only touch you if you ask me."

I bit back a sigh of relief. I was confident I wouldn't be asking the Vandar to touch me. Not when his touch made me tremble.

"But if you take my marks before the two moons align, you will commit to being my mate for life."

The laugh burst out of me, and all the raiders twisted to stare. I stopped laughing and pressed my fingers to my lips. "Sorry. The idea of me taking your marks, whatever that means, and being your mate for life is pretty farfetched, don't you think?"

"Why is that?"

Heat suffused my face. "Well, you're a badass Vandar warlord and I'm...a plain old human."

"I would hardly call you plain or old."

I looked away from his intense gaze, not used to compliments, even if it was a weak one. "Still, what are the chances of *us* happening?"

His dark eyes held mine for a beat before he tore them away. "That is up to you, Juliette."

It was the first time I remembered him saying my name, and the sound of it spoken in his velvety burr sent an unwanted shiver of desire through me.

"Do you agree to my deal?"

"That you'll take me home unless I get your marks and become your mate? Yep. I can definitely agree to that."

"Good." The ship entered the open hangar bay of the warbird and touched down. His tail tightened around my leg, the bare flesh beneath it prickling with heat. "I will hold you to your word."

I shrugged off the dark rumble of his words and the warning behind them. No problem, I thought. All I needed to do was bide my time until the moon alignment, and then I was as good as gone. There was no chance in hell I'd ever be a mate for a Raas of the Vandar.

CHAPTER ELEVEN

Vassim

The air in the warrior's canteen was smoky when I entered, raiders sucking on *targilis* and blowing the blue smoke from the Chantarian water pipes in curling plumes above their heads. It was a habit my raiders had picked up from a hedonistic planet in the hinterlands—the smoke providing a euphoria even Cressidian gin couldn't match—and I allowed them to indulge it in the canteen after shifts. Although the smoke carried the sweet scent of *narli* fruit and *gerron* leaves, I still coughed from the heady perfume that hung thick in the air and made me squint to find my *majak*.

Taan stood at the far end of the crowded room, leaning against the long ebony bar, his elbows behind him and a tankard in one hand. The buzz of my raiders' voices was so loud that he could not hear me call his name, but the crowd parted as I made my way to him through the crush of bodies. When he saw me, he straightened and clicked his heels together, as did the other raiders as I passed.

"As you were." I waved a hand toward the warrior behind the bar, motioned to my *majak's* drink so he would give me one of the same.

"I have not seen you since you returned from Qualynn, Raas."

My first officer had remained on the warbird to command while I was gone, and because he did not enjoy the unpredictable nature of the mystical planet. Ever since he'd taken one of Ferria's pleasurers to bed and she'd transformed into her natural form, complete with eight tentacles, he'd preferred to experience Qualynn from a distance.

I took the pewter tankard handed to me from behind the bar and raised it in salute. "To Vandar."

Taan lifted his own drink and repeated my words, taking a long swig and watching me do the same. "Did you not get the answer you wished? Is the female not the one from the witch's prophecy?"

The cool ale was both refreshing and thirst-quenching, and I drained half the tankard in a single gulp. "Ferria claims she is the one who has the power to break the curse."

Taan slapped a hand on my shoulder. "That is good news, Raas. Why do you not look pleased?" He lowered his voice, even though the din of the raucous laughter and loud conversation made it unnecessary. "This means you could return to a normal existence."

"It is not so simple." I clenched my hand around the cold metal of the tankard, glad it was strong enough not to shatter. "Finding her was not enough. I have until the two moons of

Vandar align. If she does not take my mating marks by then, and become my one true mate, the curse will remain."

My *majak's* mouth fell open. "You must take a human mate?"

"I am surprised you would object to that. You have always enjoyed a variety of alien females." My *majak* was known for his skill as a charmer of all kinds of females. Although he indulged in pleasurers like the rest of the crew, he also had lovers awaiting his return on almost all the planets we visited. For Taan, the chase and seduction were as enjoyable as the conquest.

Taan took a swig then wiped the foam off his lip with the back of his hand. "That is true, but none of them are my mate." His brow furrowed. "This is serious, Raas. A Vandar only has one true mate for life. How do you even know it is possible with this delicate, little human?"

Our horde might have been out of contact with the rest of the Vandar warlords, but word had still reached me of the humans my fellow Raas' had claimed. "Vandar and human matings are possible. The three Raas brothers all have human mates who have taken their marks. I saw Corvak's and his human's marks with my own eyes."

The worried look on Taan's face did not fade. "But is that what you want, Raas? I thought you found humans to be weak and cowardly. How could such a creature be the mate of a Raas such as you?"

I did not want to tell him that the same thoughts had been haunting my mind since the witch had made her pronouncement. Even if the human would free me from my torment, could I accept her as my Raisa? That was assuming she could form any type of attachment to me, a detail that seemed even more insurmountable. I remembered her soft, trembling body and her terrified eyes then chugged the rest of my ale and slammed the tankard down on the bar. "I do not know."

Taan turned and braced his arms on the bar. "You know I was never good at Vandar astronomy, but unless I'm wrong, there isn't a great deal of time until the moons align."

"There isn't," I said, forcing down the panic that fluttered in my chest. If I missed this chance to break the curse, I might indeed go insane or put myself out an airlock.

My *majak* studied me for a moment, frowning. "And you believe this witch?"

"She has never been wrong in her predictions before."

He gave a curt nod and straightened. "Then we assume she is right, and this human female is the answer."

I rubbed a hand across my forehead. "I wish the answer was something simple, like battling a herd of poisonous kerligs."

Taan laughed. "For you, that might be easier than seducing a female."

I snapped my head to him. "Seducing?"

"How do you think you will get the creature to fall for you enough to take your mating marks in so short a time?" He looked down his nose at me. "I hope you weren't counting on your natural charm to win her over."

I grunted at him. "You have a better way?"

"Every way is a better way," he muttered, then gave me another hard thump on the back. "Do not worry, Raas. You have much to recommend you to a female. We just need to show that to this human."

I beckoned for another ale, the buzz from the first one not enough to quell the nerves that were making my pulse jangle. Why did this tiny human provoke such a reaction in me? I'd been with plenty of females and none of them had awoken such primal desires. If I revealed my dominant desires to Juliette, she would run away screaming. But I didn't know if I could be as patient and charming as Taan believed I should be.

"For her to take my marks, I must claim her," I said.

"But that is not enough. How many females have we both fucked who have never taken our marks?"

"Maybe we didn't fuck them enough times," I suggested.

"It is not about frequency, Raas." The corners of his mouth quirked up. "Trust me on this one. Besides, you cannot just pounce on this female. She might faint at the sight of your cock."

I took the ale the warrior behind the bar slid to me, shaking my head. "This is impossible. I might be able to deal with a human female, but not one who is also so innocent. She comes from a peaceful planet, and has never held a weapon or seen a body fall in battle. She thinks I am a brute."

My *majak* considered my words for a moment. "Show her you are not."

"You wish me to prove I am not a bloodthirsty warlord of the Vandar who fucks as hard as he fights, even as we return to engage the Zagrath in battle?"

Once we'd left Qualynn's orbit, we'd set a course to return to the sector that contained Juliette's planet. The empire's defeat at Kimithion III was only one of many recently—all at the hands of the Vandar and our allies, so now was the time to strike hard and fast. It would be a challenge to convince the human I was not a violent warlord as we stalked and raided imperial ships, my body and my axe dripping with enemy blood.

"We could delay our mission," my *majak* said. "It might be more important for you to focus your energy on one thing."

I bristled as the thought of calling off a military mission for my own personal quest, especially one that consisted of me trying to lure a female into my bed. "What kind of Raas would do that?"

"One who needs to be rid of his torment," Taan said, his eyes holding mine. "You are not yet *lunori,* but you will be, if you cannot break the curse."

I growled, hating the truth of his words. "I will not call off the mission. We are still raider warriors of the Vandar, and I am still a warlord who is pledged to destroy the Zagrath empire."

My *majak* sighed, but nodded his understanding.

I clamped a hand on his shoulder. "But I will take any expert advice you might have for seducing females."

Taan grinned and arched an eyebrow at me, but his instruction was preempted by a warrior pushing his way through the crowd.

The young, bare-chested raider snapped his ankles sharply. "Raas, you are being urgently hailed on the command deck."

My stomach clenched. Who could be hailing me here?

CHAPTER TWELVE

Vassim

"Are you in need of assistance?" I asked the gold-skinned Dothvek on the view screen. My chest still heaved from the run from the warrior's canteen to the bridge, and my *majak* stood next to me, breathing just as heavily.

"We actually wished to offer *you* assistance," the alien called K'alvek said. On screen he looked even broader than he had in person, with dark slash marks emblazoned across both sides of his bare chest.

I tried to mask my annoyance because this warrior was an ally. And it hadn't been his fault that my warrior had been so startled by the transmission that he'd rushed to get me, causing me and my *majak* to tear out of the canteen and thunder through the warbird, leaping across suspended walkways and taking iron stairs three at a time.

It wasn't customary for Vandar to work with other warriors, but after battling the empire together on Kimithion III, I had a respect for the bounty hunter crew. They were a fierce group of fighters made up of various alien species, all with a healthy hatred of the empire. And now, their crew even contained a Vandar raider, as well as Juliette's sister, Corvak's mate. I tried not to think about Juliette, and her connection to the bounty hunters, as I listened to the Dothvek.

"We have been tracking imperial transport runs. Raiding ships isn't what we do best, but we know it's your specialty. Corvak suggested we give you the coordinates, while we track down a couple of imperial leaders who need to disappear."

A rumble of approval passed through the command deck warriors, their attention also locked onto the image of the Dothvek standing on his ship, his unusually diverse crew at their stations behind him. His human pilot stared back at us, her dark hair pulled up high, and she appeared just as fascinated by our crew as mine was of the alien and human females who served with K'alvek.

"Send them over. We'll take care of it." The Vandar were always eager for imperial ships to raid. Even as I steadied my breath, my heart beat faster at the thought of boarding an enemy ship and swarming through its corridors with our axes high.

K'alvek nodded. "We've also intercepted transmissions from the empire. Losing the fleet at the battle for Kimithion III was another blow. After the losses at Carlogia Prime and another fleet being destroyed by the three brothers' hordes, we have them on the defensive. The supply runs have increased because we suspect they're attempting to rebuild. It's crucial we don't let that happen."

My heartbeat quickened at the news. "Be assured, we won't let it."

"Corvak assured me that you wouldn't."

I considered asking to speak to the Vandar on their ship but dismissed the idea. If I didn't speak to him, I would not be intentionally hiding the fact that I had his mate's sister on board my warbird. At least, that's what I told myself.

"We will be going dark after this transmission," K'alvek said. "Our mission to track down the imperial officers requires it."

"Understood." I glanced at my communications officer at his standing console. "Do we have the coordinates from the bounty hunter ship yet?"

"Affirmative, Raas."

I turned back to the alien facing me out of the enormous screen. "We have received the coordinates and are grateful for the information."

The Dothvek nodded. "We wish you luck on your mission."

I bowed my head. "To you as well. May the gods of old bless your battle."

He grinned at me. "Goddesses." Then his face vanished from the screen, replaced by the blackness of space.

I pivoted to Taan. "Goddesses?"

"The Dothveks worship goddesses," he explained with a half shrug. "It's a religion I could get behind."

I choked back a laugh. "I have no doubt you have worshipped many goddesses already."

My *majak* gave me a wicked smile. "I like to think that every female is a goddess in her own way."

"That explains a lot."

"It's a strategy you should consider." Taan strode to his console, swiping his fingers across the surface. "Downloading the coordinates and plotting a course to intercept the nearest imperial transport, Raas. The nearest transport is an imperial freighter on a course for an outpost on Alpha 312." My *majak's* fingers danced across the screen before he looked up at me. "Laying in a course to intercept, and transmitting to all the horde ships."

"Strategy?" I asked, leading us to my private room attached to the command deck, the doors swishing open upon my approach.

"You think conquering females is so different from battle?" He shook his head, as we stepped into the long, narrow room dominated by a wall-sized star chart and a glass window overlooking space. "Both require a strategy to succeed."

"I have never approached females with a strategy."

My *majak* made a dismissive face at me. "Because you rely on pleasurers. They require no strategy, not that I haven't enjoyed the ease of their company many times. But the fact remains that they are a sure thing and not a challenge that requires advanced planning."

"Have you always approached females this way?" I braced one hand against the star chart with blinking coordinates dotting the clear surface. I'd never given much thought to my first officer's reputation as a skilled seducer of females before, only that he truly savored the company of females and the chase in acquiring it.

"Once I realized that there was no thrill of the hunt when it came to the pretty creatures in the pleasure houses, I started to study females. I schooled myself on what they liked and what they didn't, all the while learning to appreciate what was unique about each one."

"It sounds exhausting."

Taan laughed. "I have never minded being exhausted by a female."

"How have I never known this about you?" I asked, as he returned to stand next to me on the platform overlooking the command deck. "We have served together since we were apprentices."

"You never seemed interested. Besides, I didn't know all this when I was an apprentice." He nudged me with his elbow. "Back then, I was just as eager as anyone to be allowed free rein in the pleasure houses. It was a long time until I tired of the practiced looks and skilled mouths of the pleasurers."

I shuddered. "You prefer unskilled?"

He dropped his voice to a whisper. "There is nothing like a female who is eager to learn, and for whom everything is new. You are lucky, Raas, if the human female is truly as innocent as she seems."

I did not feel lucky when I thought about Juliette. Conflicting emotions roiled inside me from possessive desire to irritation that she was, indeed, so innocent. I was afraid that I would traumatize her if I acted on my primal desires, but I could barely contain my urge to provoke the arousal edged with fear that I'd seen in her eyes. I wished to both rid myself of the maddening creature and never let her go.

"I know nothing of teaching an innocent," I said, "or of restraining myself with one. I fuck like I fight, *majak*."

He let out a low whistle. "I have fought by your side. I doubt this female would be able to withstand *that*, Raas."

"Which is why this will never succeed." I leaned forward and gripped the iron railing running across the platform. "I cannot change myself for a female."

"I am not telling you to change yourself. I am advising you to show her your true self slowly."

I squeezed the iron. Patience had never been a strength of mine. "What if she does not like my true self, no matter how slowly I go?"

Taan cut his gaze to me. "You have never doubted yourself before, Raas. Even when we have rushed into battles where we were sorely outmatched. Why do you hesitate now, when the possibility of ending your torment is within your grasp?"

"The enemy I faced down without fear was never a female, and the outcome of the battle was never before dependent on my ability to make her fall for me."

"You are a Raas of the Vandar," my *majak* reminded me. "You will be victorious in all things."

"Approaching target ship, Raas," my nav officer's voice came through the intercom.

Taan and I left my strategy room and joined the officers on the command deck again, an image of a chunky, gray freighter filling the view screen.

"Prepare raiding party," I commanded.

I was not convinced I would be victorious with Juliette, but I could find glory in battle. I spun on my heel and stormed off the command deck to join the raiding party.

CHAPTER THIRTEEN

Juliette

I rolled over and flinched when my cheek hit the cold floor. Startled awake, I sat up and crawled back onto the pallet from which I'd rolled off.

"I guess I should be glad I didn't fall off a high bed," I whispered to myself, as I touched a hand to my cheek. "And that I didn't have any nightmares."

I hadn't been on the Vandar warbird for long, but my restless sleep had been punctuated by dreams in which I was constantly searching for my sister but never found her. Twice, I'd dreamed of running up the path to our cave dwelling on Kimithion III, but the path had been never-ending. I would glimpse her foot as she ran ahead of me, but no matter how fast I tried to run, I couldn't catch her. I'd woken myself calling out her name with tears streaking my cheeks.

My only consolation was that the Raas hadn't been around to witness me crying in my sleep. Although I wouldn't exactly call it a consolation that I hadn't seen Raas Vassim since we'd returned from the visit to Qualynn, it did make it easier to fulfill my end of the deal. There was zero chance of me becoming his mate if I never saw him.

It felt longer since I was alone in his quarters, but it probably hadn't been more than a day since we'd parted at the door. He'd claimed he needed to return to his command deck, but I could tell he'd been shaken by what the witch had told him.

Still, he hadn't returned, and I'd finally drifted off to sleep, awoken to find food set out on the low table, eaten, and fallen back asleep. The throaty rumble of the warship's engines had an impressive ability to lull me to sleep, although I was starting to dread my tumultuous dreams.

I crossed my legs in front of me and tugged the skirt of my dress over my knees, glancing over at the fire that burned without kindling. The fake blue flames cavorted in the air, sending shadows dancing across the floor. Something was different. I leaned over and placed a hand on the floor to feel for vibrations. There were none. The ship had stopped moving.

I swung my head toward the wall of glass. Stars no longer streaked past in the distance as we flew at speeds faster than my brain could process. We appeared to hover in space, but I saw no other ships around us. Then I remembered that Vandar hordes used invisibility shielding. There could be an entire fleet of their warbirds outside the window, and I'd never know. The thought made me look away and tug my skirt even lower.

How did the Vandar survive in space like this? It was so cold and lonely. Of course, I probably felt like that because I was the only woman and only human on a raider ship filled with dangerous warriors. For them, it was all they'd known. They weren't used to watching the suns rise each morning, the pink light peeking over shards of rock. They didn't breathe in the scent of salt water, or even the warm, yeasty aroma of baking bread. Their existence was comprised of dark spaceships and the smell of warriors fresh from battle.

I thought of the Raas before he'd bathed, his bronze skin flecked with blood and slick with sweat. I wasn't used to males who showed so much skin, and despite my shock, I'd longed to drag my fingers across the inky marks on his skin.

"Honestly, Juliette," I scolded myself, as heat filled my cheeks and pulsed between my legs. "You do not want him."

That's a lie, a little voice whispered in the back of my mind. *You shouldn't want him, but you do.*

I shook my head vigorously, as if the movement could shake the desire from me. Raas Vassim was nothing like the husband I'd always imagined I'd have—handsome and kind, a steady provider who never missed a day of work, or was late when returning home for supper. Even though there hadn't been a particular man on Kimithion III I thought would fit this bill, I'd always envisioned him being human. Not once had I dreamed of an alien mate who wore only a kilt and terrorized the empire as a feared warlord of the Vandar. Until the Vandar exile, Corvak, had come to our planet, I'd barely known anything about the violent species. Except that they were wild creatures who flew in hordes and were ruled by warlords. It was all I'd ever needed to know.

But now here I was, living on a Vandar warbird. I wasn't even being held against my will anymore. I'd made a deal with the Vandar. The easiest deal I'd ever made in my life, I reminded myself. All I had to do was run out the clock without succumbing to his charms, and he would have to return me to my home planet.

"Piece of frambolgi cake," I said, the memory of my favorite fruity dessert making my stomach growl. I couldn't exactly fall for a guy who was never around, and so far, Raas Vassim was a shadow.

Standing up, I walked over to the low table. Domes covered the plates that had been switched out while I slept, fragrant steam billowing up as I lifted first one and then another. It wasn't frambolgi cake, but the savory smells made my mouth water, nonetheless. I found a basket of warm rolls, biting into one and closing my eyes as I chewed. They weren't as sweet as the ones I made, but they were still bread. And if there was one thing I loved about almost all else, it was bread.

I missed baking more than I even missed eating my creations. The measured order of mixing up dough and rolling it onto a floured surface had always calmed me and provided a steadiness to my life, even in the midst of pain or loneliness. I'd never felt lost or alone when I was baking, and I longed to be in a kitchen and feel the heat of the ovens. I'd be back home in my kitchen soon, I reminded myself as I swallowed the Vandar bread.

I polished off two rolls before tearing off a bite of bread and dipping it into one of the stew-like dishes. The flavor was stronger than I was accustomed to—and there was no fish base to the dish, which was a trait common to Kimitherian dishes—but it was strangely addictive. I used the bread to scoop up more of it as I ate standing up, finally washing it all down with a gulp of the claret-colored beverage in the carafe.

The Vandar wine had even more of a kick than the food, making my fingers tingle after only a few swallows. But it was a welcome feeling. Besides, what else did I have to do? I'd never gotten drunk before, always avoiding the fermented algae on my home world because I'd seen what it had done to my father. But this wine tasted nothing like algae, and it made me feel light and giggly, not angry and combative like my father.

When I could no longer feel my fingers or my lips, I walked gingerly back to the pallets that served as a bed, flopping down and stretching my hands over my head. Aside from making me lightheaded, the wine stirred a sinful heat between my legs. I was so distracted by the strange sensation, I almost didn't hear the door slide open.

But I did hear Raas Vassim stomp into the room. I sat bolt upright, gaping at the Vandar with fresh streaks of blood on his chest.

CHAPTER FOURTEEN

Juliette

"What happened?" The buzz in my head disappeared as my eyes focused on his tangled hair and the wet blade of his axe, drops of something I assumed was blood splattering the floor where he stood.

"We raided an imperial ship," he said, as he took off his armor and hung it on the stand near the door.

I shook my head in an attempt to shake off the last of the wine-induced cobwebs. "Just now?" I glanced at the wall of glass. "Is that why we stopped?"

He peered at me, his gaze moving across my body without hesitation. "Have you been sleeping all this time?"

"No," I said quickly. He didn't need to know that I'd only woken up briefly to eat. Then I got defensive. What else was I supposed to do all alone in his quarters? "Not that there's anything else for me to do since you left me in here by myself."

"Would you rather I stay in bed with you?"

I clamped my mouth shut. So much for complaining. I was reminded of the Kimitherian saying, beware of your wishes.

The Raas proceeded to undress as he watched me, but he hesitated before he dropped his kilt. I averted my eyes, even though part of me—the part of me that the Vandar wine had made bold and mouthy—wanted to watch. But instead of losing the kilt, he strode toward the bathing area with it still hanging low on his hips.

As he passed me, my gaze was drawn to the wide expanse of his back, and I sucked in a sharp breath. "Your back!"

He stopped and looked over his shoulder at me. "What about my back?"

I stood and hurried to him, my eyes still locked on the open gash across his shoulder. "You can't feel it? You have a huge cut!"

He twisted his head as if he might actually be able to look at his own shoulder blade fully. "I remember getting hit in my back, but I didn't know the wound was bad."

Even though I hadn't grown up around weapons, I'd grown up with a sister who got into a lot of fights, mostly defending me from the petty comments boys would make about me having more curves than the rest of the girls. I'd become adept at patching up the cuts and bruises that Sienna would bring home, so although this cut was more significant than anything I treated, I wasn't afraid to tend to it.

"You may be a big, tough warlord, but you can't ignore this." I took his hand and pulled him into the bathing area. "Do you have any first aid supplies in here?"

"First aid?"

"Come on, you must treat wounds. I'm guessing you guys get a lot of them."

He furrowed his brow. "We have a healer, but he's rarely used for scrapes, which I'm sure this is."

For the first time, I noticed scars on his back and a few thin ones on his arms. "I wouldn't call this a scrape. At least let me clean it for you."

He twitched his shoulder and flinched slightly.

"Aha!" I wagged a finger at him. "I knew it hurt."

"The adrenaline from the fight is wearing off, that is all."

I tugged him to the long counter and flicked on one of the polished-ebony knobs over the sunken basin. Water poured out, and I used my hand as a scoop to dribble it over his cut. When I was content that it was clean, I glanced around the pristine room. No stacks of towels. No robes. Nothing.

"I should dry this, but I guess Vandar raiders don't believe in towels?"

He nodded to the far wall that held a square post covered with metal button embedded in the shiny stone. "We dry ourselves with pressurized air."

Every time I thought the Vandar were barbarians, they impressed me with their technology. "I don't think pressurized air would be good for your cut."

"What would be good for my wound is a bath."

Before I could argue with him that I doubted the perfumed water would be a good idea for an open cut, he turned away from me and dropped his kilt. My mouth went dry as my gaze followed the blood-stained kilt to the floor. I didn't have much time to admire his ass before he walked over to the segmented pools and turned again, lowering himself into the murky green water. Once he was submerged, I couldn't see him, but I'd gotten enough of a look for my mouth to go dry. Not only was his cock long and thick, but it also carried the same swirling black lines as his chest.

Gaping at him like a widemouthed Jer-Jer fish gasping for air wasn't doing anything to make me look less clueless, but I couldn't help it. I'd never seen anyone like Raas Vassim, and I'd definitely never known anyone who was so comfortable being naked. Flashes of skin were rare on my home world, partially because of the two suns and the damage they could do to unprotected flesh, and partly because the native Kimitherians had a strict morality code that frowned on exposure of anything more than an ankle or wrist. Even an uncovered collarbone was considered risqué.

But Raas Vassim had no such qualms. Not that he should. His body looked like it had been sculpted out of stone. My fingertips hummed with the desire to touch the naked skin that was now submerged under the green water. I clasped my hands in front of me and jerked my gaze away, my cheeks burning at the forbidden thoughts flooding my mind. Thoughts I couldn't have if I was going to get off his ship and back to my home.

I took a step back toward the arched doorway. "I'm going to go and let you bathe."

"No need." As swiftly as he'd lowered himself neck deep into the pool, he straightened and stepped out.

Water streamed off his body, pooling on the floor as he strode to the stone pillar covered in buttons. Before I could think to avert my eyes, I noticed that the cut on his back was significantly smaller.

"Your gash," I said, pointing to the red slash that was already fading to pink. "It's…"

"Our bathing pools are not only for pleasure." He stood in front of the black pillar and pressed a button. Air rushed up from the floor, evaporating the remaining water on his body and warming the room a few degrees. He flicked off the air. "They can heal, increase stamina, and elicit the truth."

I glanced at the vividly hued waters, wondering which color contained which power, aside from the green that could clearly hasten healing. "More magic?"

The Raas shook his head as he walked toward me. "No magic. Only herbs that grew on the home world of Vandar. They are one of the old-world traditions we maintain."

As fascinated as I was by this knowledge, I was also very aware that he was now standing in front of me wearing nothing. I fought to keep my gaze high and my furious blush under control. "Like your kilts?"

He watched me, a smile teasing the corner of his mouth. "Like our battle kilts and our axes." He cupped my face in one hand, brushing the pad of his thumb over my scalding cheek. "And our mating marks."

My heart hammered wildly as he closed the small gap between us, and I bit my bottom lip to keep from gasping when something hard bumped against my stomach.

"Would you like to know how females get our mating marks?" he husked, the rumble of his voice a caress that skimmed across my flesh and made my knees go weak.

I was saved from answering or making a pathetic squeaking noise by the door to his quarters beeping.

Raas Vassim's molten gaze shuttered, and he stepped back. "*Vaes*," he commanded as he strode out of the bathroom. "I have something for you."

I allowed myself to sag against the counter once he was in the adjoining room as it truly hit me how in over my head I was. Then the boom of the Raas' voice made me jump.

"*Vaes!*"

CHAPTER FIFTEEN

Vassim

After retrieving a swath of clean fabric from a drawer, I strode to the door. My pulse raced from standing so close to Juliette and witnessing her reaction to me. Her fear was almost completely replaced by arousal, and it was clear she was battling her desire as much as I was. I pushed down my aching cock, trying to think of anything but the female in the next room.

"*Vaes!*" I called out as the door beeped again.

The metal seam of the arched door opened, and one of my warriors stepped inside holding a squirming ball of golden fluff out as far away from his body as possible. Still, there were abrasions on his chest from the spiky tail that was swinging wildly. "The Gerwyn has been decontaminated, Raas."

What had seemed like a good idea when we'd found the shipment of exotic pets on the imperial freighter, I now questioned. "You may set it down."

The warrior lowered it to the floor so quickly, he almost dropped it. The alien creature immediately scampered away from him and toward the sleeping pallets.

"It injured you?" I asked, eyeing the cuts on my raider's chest.

The warrior didn't spare them a glance. "Nothing that I noticed, Raas. The beast does use his tail for defense, though. At least his teeth are not sharp."

I grunted as the puffy animal burrowed itself under a cushion.

"The Zagrath keep these as pets?" the raider who'd delivered him asked.

"Apparently." The Gerwyn hadn't been the only animal being shipped to the imperial outpost. From the large number of exotic animals in the hold, I suspected the empire did a bustling trade in unusual pets for its indulged population.

When I'd seen the little animal cowering in its cell, I'd immediately thought of Juliette. At the time, bringing her a gift from the raiding mission had seemed like a gesture worthy of Taan. Now that the alien pet was in my quarters, however, it seemed impulsive and foolish. I didn't even know if the human liked animals.

Juliette emerged from the bathing chamber, her cheeks less pink than they had been. When she spotted me by the door with one of my raiders, her brow furrowed in curiosity.

My raider clicked his heels together when Juliette appeared. "If there is nothing else you require, Raas?"

I dismissed him and scanned the space for the Gerwyn.

"Is everything okay?" Juliette asked.

Folding the fabric around my waist down a few times so it wouldn't slip, I beckoned her to the pallets. "I have something for you."

She hesitated, her gaze dipping below my waist.

I quickly crossed my hands over my bulge. *"That* is not it."

She didn't look convinced, so I dug around beneath the cushions until my hands brushed something furry and quivering. Being careful to hold the tail with my other hand, I pulled up the Gerwyn and held it out to her.

Her eyebrows popped up. "What is that?"

I glanced at the wiggling, golden puff as I attempted to keep it from leaping out of my hands. "It's a Gerwyn. The Zagrath keep them as pets. They're said to be very enjoyable."

Juliette's mouth trembled and she pressed her lips together.

"Are you laughing?"

She slapped a hand over her mouth, shaking her head as she shook with obvious laughter. "It's just that you don't look like you're enjoying yourself very much. It looks like you're trying to subdue a sea eel."

Her laugh was infectious, and I couldn't keep a chuckle from slipping out of me. "Maybe I should have asked first if you wanted a pet."

"Here." She reached for the creature, and I gladly handed it over. Instead of struggling in her arms, the Gerwyn went limp and allowed her to stroke its head. Or at least, what I thought might be his head. There was so much fur it was impossible to tell.

After a few moments, the fur relaxed, and the tiny creature beneath was revealed, his eyes wide and his whiskers twitching as he looked up at Juliette.

She rubbed behind his ears and one of his back legs jiggled. "He looks a bit like a puppy."

"A puppy?"

"A pet that humans had on Earth. They still have them on some colonies, but I've only seen images." She peered at me. "Where did you get this guy?"

"On our raiding mission. The empire does a big business in trapping exotic creatures and selling them as pets. Most of the cargo on the ship we raided was exotic creatures."

"So you rescued him?"

I jerked one shoulder up. "I thought you might enjoy the company."

"What about the other creatures?"

"In our hold being tended to by my raiders, who are none too happy about it. We are returning them to the planet from where they were taken and releasing them. It's a diversion, but I cannot keep them in my hold for long."

She tilted her head at me. "I thought Vandar raiders blew up imperial cargo ships."

"We do not murder innocent creatures, no matter what the Zagrath claim about us." I pivoted away from her and walked to the low table, pouring myself a glass of wine and gulping it down.

"I'm sorry. I didn't mean to suggest you would. I guess I should have learned by now that the Vandar aren't what I thought they'd be. Corvak already proved that he would fight for our planet when he didn't have to, and you're supposed to be the scariest Raas, but you go around rescuing boys from pleasure houses and animals being taken from their homes."

The wine seared my throat and warmed my belly. So, she'd been talking to Baru. "You do not believe I am scary anymore?"

"I wouldn't want to make you angry, but you don't frighten me anymore, no."

I put down the empty goblet and flopped down on the nearest pallet, the battle, bath, and wine making my movements sluggish and my eyes even heavier than usual. "It would be a mistake to underestimate how dangerous I can be, especially to you."

Juliette lowered herself onto the edge of the pallet and set the Gerwyn down beside her. "Because you're Raas, and can do anything you wish?"

I interlaced my hands behind my head and watched her. "No, although both of those things are true. I am dangerous because I can show you a side of yourself you didn't know existed, and one you might not want to give up."

She frowned at me, a wrinkle forming between her eyes. "I don't know what you're talking about. I'll be very happy when you return me to my home planet like you promised."

"You will wish to return to that dull, restrictive world after you've seen what exists beyond?"

"It's not dull," she said, her shrill tone making the Gerwyn flinch, and its fur fluff up again.

"You would prefer a long existence that never changes, over the adventure of life in space?" Since I'd spent my life on a horde ship, a never-changing planet seemed like slow torture.

"Space is dangerous, especially the way you live out here." She shook her head and her curls bobbled around her face. "You've already been wounded."

"Any life worth living has risks. If you aren't scared every so often, you aren't really living."

"Spoken like a Vandar," she muttered, rubbing the Gerwyn's belly when he rolled over. "Some of us don't like being scared all the time."

I sat up and leaned close to her, curling my tail around her waist. "What about some of the time?"

She lifted her chin. "You don't scare me."

I lifted her hand and turned it over so that the pale skin of her wrist was exposed. I pressed a kiss to it, the pulse fluttering madly under my lips. "It isn't wise to lie to a Raas."

"I'm not lying." Her eyes were dark, the pupils dominating the paler ring of blue. "I know you won't hurt me. I've seen the heart beneath the steel."

Juliette did not understand the two sides of the Vandar, and how my compassion did not make me any less violent and deadly to my enemies. Nor did it quench my desire to dominate her and claim her body as mine. I wanted to be tender with her, like my *majak* had advised, but I also wanted to throw her back and bury myself between her soft thighs. Conflicting desires stormed within me and I fought to control them.

I forced her fist open and placed another kiss on her skin, this one on her palm. "You should not be afraid of me hurting you, Juliette. You should be afraid of the opposite. You should be afraid of me giving you so much pleasure you never want to leave me." I licked her palm with the tip of my tongue. "I *will* make you scream and beg me for more."

She snatched her hand away from me. "That's not going to happen."

Her words were sharp, but her voice wavered. The Gerwyn was oblivious to the tension crackling between us as he sniffed around us, finally curling up on the cushion beside me.

I lay back and let my eyes close. "We will see."

CHAPTER SIXTEEN

Juliette

I curled up as far as I could get from the sleeping Raas. His words had made it impossible to sleep. How could he possibly think that I'd want him to make me scream and would be begging him for more? That was the last thing I wanted.

I focused on the shadows dancing on the dark ceiling, the flames from the eternal fire sending a warm glow across the room, even if they didn't make it any warmer. I missed my small bedroom in our dwelling on Kimithion III, with its single bed and heavy blanket across the foot. The wide-open space of the Raas' quarters were the opposite of cozy, even if they were more luxurious and the blankets covering me made of silky furs. I didn't care about the cool Vandar tech, or even their healing pools. No matter how much more sophisticated life was on the horde ship, it would never be home. And nothing the Raas could say would change that, even if he did make my pulse race and heat coil in my core.

I huffed out a breath and turned away from him. Even though I knew he was completely wrong about me and well, everything, I still couldn't fall asleep. His tossing and turning wasn't helping either. Even though the Raas had fallen asleep quickly, his breath deepening almost as soon as he'd closed his eyelids, he'd almost instantly started to twitch in his sleep.

The Gerwyn I'd decided to name Furb had retreated away from the Vandar, and was now sleeping in a ball near my feet. I didn't blame him. The Raas was not a peaceful sleeper, and his thick legs could crush something as small as the fur ball if they kicked out too wildly.

"No!" The Vandar's scream made me almost scurry off the bed after Furb, who'd woken and run on his little legs all the way to the corner of the room.

When I sat up and peered through the dark room at the Raas, he was no longer twitching in his sleep. He was thrashing, as if he were being stung by a pod of electric sea eels. His legs moved almost as if he were running in place, and he swung his arms like he was holding a weapon. Even in the shadowy light from the fire, it was obvious that sweat was running down his face, which was set in a tortured grimace.

"Raas!" The pain in his cry made my stomach clench and my heart squeeze. I'd had bad dreams before, but this was on a whole different level.

I didn't know if it was safe to wake him, but I couldn't bear watching him suffer. I tentatively shook his shoulder, dodging his flailing arms. "Raas, wake up. You're dreaming."

But he didn't wake. Instead, he sat up and pulled me to him, cradling me as he wailed. The hairs on the back of my neck prickled as he moaned over me, clearly thinking that I was someone else. I tried to wiggle away, but his grip was too tight, so I tried a different approach.

"Vassim," I said over his moaning. "Vassim, wake up!"

The sound of his name did something. He stilled, his eyes flying open. He blinked down at me, clearly not sure why he was holding me.

He loosed his grip. "What's—?"

"You were having a nightmare. I tried to wake you."

He pulled back like he'd been burned, and I moved back to my side of the pallet. Staring down at his hands, he asked, "Did I hurt you?"

"No, but I was afraid you might hurt yourself."

He shook his head. "It is never me who gets hurt."

"You've had bad dreams before?"

He rubbed a hand over his brow. "All of my dreams are tormented. It's my curse."

I stared at him for a moment as the words sunk in. "This is your curse? To have bad dreams? This is what we went to the witch about?"

He reached for the nearly empty carafe of wine, slugging it straight from the container. When it was empty, he put it back and glanced at me. "They are not just any bad dreams. Every time I fall asleep, I'm forced to relive the battle in which my former Raas was killed. I experience all the sensations as if I were back on the battlefield, including the agony of not reaching my Raas in time to save him. But the curse doesn't allow me any deviation, so each time I believe I might reach him in time and each time he dies in my arms."

Silence stretched between us as I absorbed the horror of his fate.

"That would be torture enough, but the alien who placed the curse on me also made it so that I wake up feeling like I never slept, the exhaustion of the battle and the aches of my body just as fresh as they were that day."

"So you never get any rest, no matter how much you sleep?" I couldn't imagine how he'd been living with such a curse, but now I understood why he was so desperate to end it. "No wonder they call you deranged." As soon as I uttered the words, I regretted them. "I'm sorry. I didn't mean that."

"No, you are right. They do call me *Lunori* Raas because I walk the ship at all hours to keep from sleeping, sometimes talking to myself to stay awake. Even my raiders fear what will happen when the madness overtakes me."

I glanced at the spikes on the walls and strange contraptions that seemed to me to be torture devices. "That is what those are for? To keep you awake?"

He followed my gaze and flinched, as if remembering the pain of using them. "Yes, but even agony can't chase away my sleep forever."

I scooted closer to him. "How long has it been?"

"So many rotations I've lost count." He raked a hand through his long hair. "My body survives because it does restore itself enough, even though I never feel like it does. Another cruel twist of the curse."

I thought back to our visit to the mystical planet. "And the witch couldn't remove the curse?"

He moved his head back and forth slowly. "Only the witch or warlock who casts it may remove it completely, and the Porvakian warlock who cursed me is long dead."

"The curse didn't die with him?"

"Not this one. It was cast with his dying breath. Ferria was able to unravel its cure, but only in parts."

I swallowed hard as I remembered that *I* was the cure. "That's why you had to bring me to see her?"

He grunted, not meeting my gaze. "Once she determined you fit the requirements, she could unravel the rest of the cure. But not without something from you. The magic was shrouded too carefully for any other way to work."

"How did the warlock who cursed you come up with such a strange way to break the curse?"

The Raas let out a low, mirthless laugh. "He knew the Vandar well. I have no doubt he believed that the chances of a violent Raas who lived far away from the civilized galaxy finding a fair, pure female and making her his one true mate were very slim. It was his way of ensuring I was never free of his torture."

The story was so far-fetched that I might have thought he was making it all up if I hadn't seen how physically he'd reacted to his nightmare and how seriously the shapeshifting witch had taken her spellcraft.

"Why didn't you tell me all this earlier?"

He finally met my eyes. "Would you have believed me?"

The Raas had a point. Even though I did believe that he was tormented by horrible nightmares that were more real than anything I'd experienced, that didn't mean I could force myself to fall in love with him. I still didn't understand about the Vandar mating marks he mentioned, or how they picked their one true mate, but just like he'd said before, I was not Vandar mate material.

All I wanted was to go home and forget about the Raas and his terrifying dreams, and the dark warbird that raided and pillaged everywhere it went. The life of a Vandar wasn't for me, and I definitely wasn't for him.

"I'm sorry," I said softly. I wasn't telling him I was sorry about his nightmarish curse. I was telling him that I was sorry I couldn't help him. Not if it meant sacrificing myself and my future. After spending all of my life taking care of my father and even my older sister, I couldn't give up the only thing I had left —myself—to someone I barely knew.

The Raas stood and walked across to the inset cabinets, pulling out a fresh kilt and stepping into it while the fabric slipped to the floor. Then he strode to the stand near the door, stepping into his boots and hooking his axe on his belt. When the door swished open, he hesitated on the threshold, facing away from me. "It is I who am sorry. You deserve better than me, Juliette, and better than being pulled into this cruel game."

Then he left without looking back at me.

CHAPTER SEVENTEEN

Vassim

"Again!"

My *majak* stood across the battle ring from me with his hands braced on his knees. We were both breathing heavily, but he had the advantage of a night's sleep, which I did not. My side twinged as I sucked in a breath, and I swiped at the sweat dripping into my eyes.

"Are you sure, Raas?"

I shook out my arms, even though they felt like lead. "Again!"

Taan sighed and rushed at me once more, leaping up and grasping the chain link of the cage enclosing the circular practice ring. I spun and jumped back but he was already flying through the air toward me. Diving forward, I barely escaped being tackled, and I somersaulted across the ring and popped up on the other side, spinning quickly.

There was one thing I could always count on from my *majak*—he would not go easy on me. If I called him to join me in the battle ring, he knew I needed him to fight me like he would any opponent. I couldn't bear to be treated differently by the one warrior who knew me better than any.

I grinned at him after he'd dive-rolled across the floor and leapt up again. "You always were an excellent jumper."

"If only we did battle on terrain that consisted of metal caging." He bent low and swayed from side to side, returning my grin.

I straightened and blew out a long breath. "Enough. Let's drink."

Taan unhooked a metal canister from the caging and tossed it to me. "Will this do, or did you have something harder in mind?"

I took a swig of the cool water and shook my head. "The last thing I need is something else to muddle my head."

My first officer drank from his own canister, holding it high and letting the stream of water arc into his mouth. "Another dream?"

I choked back a laugh. "If only they were dreams, my friend."

He frowned, his frustration evident. If I was his *majak*, I would have felt the same way—helpless to aid my Raas. I knew the sensation all too well.

He opened the door to the cage and stepped back for me to precede him from the ring. "At least you have a chance to end it. You found the female when you didn't believe it possible, and you'd given up all hope."

I growled as I thought back to Juliette's face as she'd told me she was sorry. She'd felt something for me, but it hadn't been what I wanted her to feel. I didn't want her pity, and I couldn't stand the idea of her feeling sorry for me.

"I never should have told her," I murmured under my breath, stomping down the short flight of stairs and tossing the empty canister as far as I could, the metal clanging against the hard floor as it landed.

"What did you tell her, Raas?"

I faced the ring and curled my fingers around the metal caging, welcoming the bite of the steel into my flesh as I squeezed. "She witnessed me reliving the battle in my sleep. When she tried to wake me, I grabbed her."

"Is she hurt?"

I swung my head to him, glowering. "Of course not." I looked away. "But in my tortured state, I believed her to be our Raas. I was holding her when I finally awoke. She looked petrified."

Taan didn't speak.

"I had to explain what had happened."

"You told her everything?"

I nodded, staring forward into the empty ring. "She deserved to know."

"This is good, Raas. Now she understands why she's so important and why she must stay."

I sagged, letting my body hang from my fingers. "That is not how the curse works. I cannot force her. She must take my mating marks of her own free will."

"But if she knows what is at stake," he said, his voice hopeful. "If she has seen what the curse does to you, surely—"

"She can sacrifice herself for my comfort?" I asked, cutting him off as I narrowed my gaze at him. "Because that is what I am asking of her, a sacrifice of everything she has ever known to save a stranger."

Taan square his shoulders as if facing off against me in battle. "You are not a stranger. You are a Raas of the Vandar. You rule over hundreds of raiders and are responsible for the destruction of many imperial ships and the salvation of enslaved planets. Maybe it is a sacrifice, but it is a worthy one."

"That isn't for us to decide."

My *majak* did not back down. "I will talk to her. She might only be a human, but surely she can understand the gravity of your situation."

"No," I snapped, standing tall again. "I forbid it."

I'd already revealed my weakness to Juliette and seen the pity in her eyes. I would not have my *majak* beg for me. She might feel sympathy for me, but so far, the only other emotion she had shown for me except fear was a flicker of primal arousal that my naked body had provoked. That alone would not create a bond strong enough to form mating marks. As Taan had said before, if fucking produced mating marks, the galaxy would be littered with pleasurers marked by Vandar raiders. Not to mention that Taan alone would have marked half the galaxy's females who were not pleasurers.

"Fine." Taan grunted his assent. "I will not go against your wishes, but did you take any of my advice regarding the female?"

"Yes and no."

Taan groaned. "What does that mean?"

"I presented her with a gift like you suggested."

His eyes lit up. "A sweet that you could feed her?"

"No, a Gerwyn from the raiding mission."

My *majak* stared at me, his expression like stone. "Do you mean the furry creatures with spiky tails? You gave one of those as a gift to woo your potential mate?"

"I thought she would like something to keep her company. The creatures only use their tails when they're agitated."

"Well, that's a relief. I can't imagine any reason for getting agitated on a Vandar warbird."

I ignored his comment. "Juliette seemed pleased with the gift."

"But you weren't able to use it to seduce her like you would have if you'd offered her sugared lomi berries. They are so juicy that it's impossible to feed them to a female without some dripping on her, which you could have licked off."

I cocked my head at Taan. "How much lomi berry juice have you licked off females?"

Now he ignored my comment. "I appreciate that you are not used to seducing females, but you do not have time to waste, Raas. The moons are getting closer to alignment all the time."

"You think I don't know that?" I tempered my voice and put a hand on my *majak's* back. "I give you my word I will try your lomi berry idea next time."

Even though Taan smiled as we walked away from the battle ring, resignation washed over me. I wasn't worthy to be cured of my torment, no matter what Juliette felt for me. I'd failed my Raas, and all the lomi berries in the world couldn't change that fact.

I just wished I didn't feel an ache in my chest and fluttering in my stomach every time I looked at her. I feared that my madness would consume me when I finally had to let her go.

CHAPTER EIGHTEEN

Juliette

"You changed," The Neebix boy, Baru, grinned as he appraised the knee-length dress I'd dug out of a bottom drawer. It was made of a much sheerer fabric than I'd ever worn before, but I could get used to the feel of the soft fabric on my skin. Not that I would admit that out loud.

"Oh, right." I glanced quickly at the blue dress. "That isn't what I wanted to talk to you about."

"Well, it looks good on you. You could almost pass for a pleasurer." He tilted his head at me. "If you did your hair up."

"A pleasurer?" I touched a hand to the shimmery fabric. "That's where these clothes came from?"

He nodded as if this was the most normal thing in the world. "Back when pleasure ships would dock with ours. The old Raas had a favorite Doloran pleasurer who kept clothes here. Raas

Vassim never bothered to clear them out when he took over as Raas."

So, I was dressed like a space whore. Just great. I shook my head, dismissing my worries. No one from my home world could see me, and the dress was by far the prettiest thing I'd ever worn. I decided I didn't care. At least the pleasurer had good taste, and I wasn't stuck in my dirty old dress.

"What did you wish to talk about, if not your new dress?" Baru asked. He'd deposited the tray of food he'd been tasked to bring me and stood holding his tail in one hand, a habit he had when something concerned him.

"I want to thank the Raas for my gift." I gestured to Furb as he scuttled across the glossy floor.

Baru did not look convinced that the ball of fur was actually a gift. "The Raas gave you that as a gift?"

"It's a Gerwyn," I told him, as if I knew anything but the name of the creature.

"And you wish to do something to thank Raas Vassim for bringing you this…"

"Furb," I said, scooping him up and stroking one hand down his head. "I've named him Furb. And yes, I want to bake something for the Raas as a thank you."

I didn't say that I also wanted to make something for the Raas because I felt guilty that I couldn't help him. More accurately, I wouldn't help him. Sweet breads wouldn't make up for that, but it was the only way I could think of to show the Vandar some kindness that didn't include me giving up my entire life.

I hadn't been able to think of much else since I'd learned of his torment, but I also hadn't been able to reconcile myself to the idea of life as a Vandar mate. Not only did I barely know him, but he wasn't even close to the husband I'd always imagined for myself, or the peaceful family life I'd craved. I hated knowing I had the power to help him and wouldn't, but the sacrifice was too much. Not when my life had already been filled with sacrifice.

Baru glanced at the domes of food on the low table. "You don't find the food satisfactory?"

"It's fine, but I love to bake. You could say that it's my passion. I want to bake something for the Raas—one of my specialties." I put my wiggling pet back on the floor. "Do you think you could arrange for me to use the kitchens?"

Now his slightly concerned expression became alarmed. "You wish to use the Vandar ovens?" He shook his head and looked down, wringing the furry tip of his tail. "I don't know about that. The cook doesn't like visitors in his kitchen."

I wondered if the Vandar cook was as intimidating as the rest of the warriors—or more. "Just take me to the kitchens, and I'll talk to him. I promise you won't get in trouble." I grinned at him. "And I'll let you taste everything I make."

His scowl softened. "I don't know."

"If he says no, I promise I won't ask again."

Baru released a loud breath and his tail. "Fine, but don't say I didn't warn you about the cook."

I clapped my hands and bent to retrieve Furb.

"No Gerwyn." Baru said. "Unless you want him to end up a stew."

I gulped and straightened. "You're kidding, right?"

The boy shrugged. "Vandar cooks have been known for getting creative when voyages run long."

That sounded ominous. I gave Furb a pat on the head as he scurried by my feet and followed Baru from the Raas' quarters. I hadn't been out of the suite since we'd returned from Qualynn, and I'd been a bit dazed then, but the warbird hummed with an energy it hadn't before.

"What's going on?" I asked as a group of raiders rushed by us, their thundering boots making the metal walkway tremble.

"Nothing out if the ordinary. This is what's it usually like when we're raiding. The Raas has been intercepting lots of imperial cargo ships, so the raiding missions have been steady. Just like the Vandar like it."

Booming voices echoed through the shadows of the ship, and I peered over the side of a spiraling staircase to the cavernous depths below. In a small way, the Vandar warbird reminded me of the cave dwellings on my home planet, the mountain path curving up from the ground with compartments shooting off from it. Of course, this ship was much larger, and while our planet was brightly lit by two suns, the Vandar preferred to be bathed in darkness.

A raider leapt down the entire length of the stairs, landing at the bottom, his kilt flying up around him. Another yelled something and barked out a laugh, also leaping down and landing with a boom that rattled my teeth.

"Another imperial ship has been sighted." Baru gripped the railings of the stairs. "A mission is leaving from the hangar bay."

"Will the Raas go on this mission?"

"Maybe yes, maybe no. He doesn't have to go on all of them, and some Raas' don't go on any, but our Raas likes to join his raiders in battle."

More bare-chested warriors barreled past us, most barely glancing at me. They were too excited about their mission to pay much notice to a female and a Neebix boy, even if we were anomalies on the ship.

"This way." Baru pulled me by the arm down a corridor that was not crowded with battle-hungry warriors.

We went down a wide set of stairs and through a hallway that looked like a tunnel. Then we were entering a space that wasn't nearly as dimly lit as the rest of the ship. The kitchen, like the rest of the ship, was mostly metal, but it was shiny and gleaming. And where the cavernous warbird was generally cool and drafty, this space billowed with heat.

"*Qu vadris?*"

Baru twitched a bit at the sharp voice, turning to the approaching Vandar.

"No problem," the boy said. "But the lady wished to speak to you."

The Vandar cook strode toward us, and he didn't appear pleased. Like all Vandar, he was huge and broad. But this alien's face was lined, and he was not bare chested. He wore a kilt, but it was made from a rough, brown fabric, and over that he wore a tunic that was splattered with evidence of his cooking. Silver shot through his dark hair, which he wore pulled back in a low ponytail.

He stopped in front of me and crossed his thick arms. "You wish to speak to me?" Although he'd spoken Vandar earlier, he now spoke the universal tongue flawlessly.

My heart raced as the Vandar towered over me, looking every bit as menacing as the raiders who'd been rushing toward battle. He didn't have an axe hanging by his side, but the knife in his hand looked equally deadly.

I drew in a breath and squared my shoulders. "I would like to use your kitchens."

His dark eyes narrowed, but before he could speak, I added, "I wish to make something special for the Raas. As a gift."

He slid his gaze to Baru and then back to me. "You are a cook?"

"I bake. Mostly breads and sweets." I steadied my breath and slowed my words before I rambled on. "I would like to make a special dessert for the Raas as a thank you."

The cook eyed me with suspicion. "Is this some sort of human mating ritual."

I wanted to balk that I was not trying to mate with the Raas, but I stilled my tongue. Even a surly cook wouldn't want to stand in the way of his Raas mating. "It is. I wish to prepare a special mating dish."

Baru shifted next to me, either uncomfortable that I was lying or uncomfortable that I wasn't.

The Vandar cook grunted. "You may have one stove, and you must stay out of my way. I still have hungry raiders to feed."

I stifled a satisfied grin, nodding instead. "Thank you. I'm sure the Raas will be grateful, as well."

He gave me a quick once-over but didn't smile. Maybe he didn't understand why the Raas would be interested in mating with a female like me. If so, he wasn't the only one.

It's only because you can break his curse, I reminded myself.

I doubted very much that a gorgeous, powerful Raas would willfully choose a shy human with too many curves and no experience.

I pushed those thoughts away. Despite what I'd told the cook, I wasn't here to whip up an aphrodisiac as a part of a human mating ritual. As far as I knew, there weren't human mating rituals, at least none that required special foods. Then again, mating wasn't ever discussed on my home world so what did I know?

Mating ritual or not, I was going to fix something special for the Raas. Something that would let him know that I was grateful for his kindness. It wouldn't make up for what I refused to give him, but it would be better than nothing, right?

I turned to Baru. "Where are the flour and sugar?"

CHAPTER NINETEEN

Vassim

My shoulder twinged as I pressed the panel to open the door to my quarters. It had been a valiant raiding battle, but the frequency with which we were boarding imperial ships was giving me little time to recuperate between battles. I welcomed a soak in the mineral waters to heal my aches.

When the door slid open, I breathed in an unexpected scent. Instead of the faint perfume drifting in from the bathing chamber, the air was sweet and yeasty. I stepped inside and let the doors shut behind me, scanning the room and locking on Juliette sitting next to the table.

"You're awake." I'd been on back-to-back raiding missions, so I wasn't sure how many watch cycles had passed, or if I should be sleeping or waking. The Gerwyn was curled up on one of the cushions, appearing almost like a round, furry pillow himself.

"I waited up for you."

My heart rate, which had just recently slowed from its fighting pace, quickened at the sight of her, pale curls spilling over her shoulders, the gossamer blue dress clinging by thin straps. The last time I'd seen her, she'd made it clear that she couldn't be what I wanted her to be. So what was this?

"I wanted to thank you," she continued, the words spilling from her in a nervous rush. "For my gift."

She stayed awake to thank me for the Gerwyn. My excitement faded as I shed my shoulder armor and belt, then hooked my battle axe on the stand and kicked off my boots. "You owe me no thanks."

I took long steps to the bathing chamber, not glancing at her again. I should not have returned to my quarters. It was too painful to be around her and know that she had no desire to be with me. I would bathe and leave, keeping myself awake in the canteen, or perhaps the battle ring, instead of using the devices in my quarters. "Go to sleep, Juliette. You should not have stayed awake for me."

When I reached the bathing pools, I dropped my kilt and stepped into the green water, the minerals tingling as I submerged myself to my chin. I leaned my head against the stone ledge and stretched my arms across it, letting my body float and my muscles uncoil. Soaking in the waters with my eyes closed, I could almost forget the human female in the other room who would not be mine.

When water splashed across my face, I spluttered and sat up, wiping my face and blinking. Juliette stood on the edge of the pool with her hands on her hips and one foot dripping wet.

"Are you always this unappreciative, or is being a jerk just a Vandar thing?" Her eyes blazed as she stared at me.

"What are you talking about?"

She waved an arm toward the other room. "I'm talking about the fact that I made you a gift to thank you for giving me Furb, and you didn't even look at it. You just stomped into your bath and ignored me."

I scraped a hand through my damp hair, trying to decipher her angry torrent of words. "You made me a gift?"

Pink mottled her cheeks, and she folded her arms tightly across her chest without responding.

I'd lived my life surrounded by males—Vandar males—so I did not understand female emotions or humans, but it was easy to see that in my attempt to avoid her and save myself pain, I'd hurt her. "I did not expect you to be awake or to make me something. I am unaccustomed to having a female in my quarters. I am used to returning from raiding missions and collapsing."

Her shoulders dropped, and she unclenched her fists. "You're in the green water again. Did you get hurt?"

I shook my head. "I am not as young a Raas as I used to be, and it has been long since we have raided non-stop like this. The aches will fade."

She bit her lower lip. "I'm sorry I flipped out on you. I guess I got too excited and didn't think that you'd be exhausted from fighting all day."

"Flipped out?"

She gave me a shy smile. "It's an Earth phrase my sister liked to use. Vintage Earth slang was a hobby of hers. It means I overreacted."

"I am the one who is sorry." Even as I said it, I was struck by the fact that I was apologizing to a human. As a Raas, I never apologized—to anyone. But I was apologizing to Juliette, and I meant it. "I would like to see what you made if you still wish to give it to me."

Her gaze went to the floor. "It isn't anything fancy, but I thought—"

I stepped out of the pool and walked to the drying vents, pressing a button and letting the warm air whoosh up around my feet. When I was dry, I turned but found that Juliette was no longer in the room. Then I remembered human's embarrassment at bare flesh.

I proceeded to the bedroom, grabbing a length of fabric to wrap around my waist and joining her on the pallet next to the table. Her gaze was locked on the domes covering the table, but she let out a breath when she glimpsed the cloth around my waist.

"Like I said, it isn't anything elaborate, and I couldn't find all the ingredients I usually use, but I thought you might enjoy it."

"You cooked?"

She lifted one of the domes to reveal a stack of puffy, golden-brown rolls covered in sparkling granules. "I baked."

Aside from the bread knots that were served with some meals and the flat bread we used to scoop up our stews, Vandar cuisine consisted of little bread, and almost nothing sweet.

"Close your eyes," she said.

"I have never closed my eyes while eating. Is this a human custom?"

"It's what you do when you're tasting a surprise."

I couldn't argue with that. I had never tasted anything that would be considered a surprise. Reluctantly, I closed my eyes.

"Now open your mouth," she ordered.

I remembered what Taan had said about seducing females with food. These breads did not seem like they would drip on us, but I could try something else. "Only if you sit on my lap."

"What?" Her voice was hesitant.

"You have your rules. I have mine." I opened my eyes slightly and pulled her so that she was sitting sideways on my lap. "Besides, it will make it easier for you to feed me your surprises."

"Okay," she gave me a small smile, "but eyes closed and mouth open."

I did as she requested, shifting her weight on me so that she wouldn't feel my cock twitch to life. Before I could think too long about how good she felt on me, she was pushing a bite between my lips.

"Now chew."

Her order was superfluous, as I was already eagerly devouring the yeasty sweet bread. It was both richly savory and sweet, the combination of flavors delicious. I kept my eyes closed as I husked out, "More."

She gave me another bite, this one of a crackling bread that was even sweeter, crumbs shattering on my lips as I bit down. I moaned as I swallowed.

"You like them?"

I opened my eyes to see her beaming at me. "I've never tasted anything like it before."

"I noticed that the Vandar aren't big into dessert, but I thought that if anyone deserved a treat it would be you."

No one had ever told me that I deserved something like a "treat," which wasn't even a word that existed in Vandar. "No one has ever made me something like this before."

"Never? Not even on your birthday?"

I tilted my head at her. "Vandar do not celebrate the day of our birth. We will celebrate a battle, but with ale, not treats like this."

"That's too bad."

I agreed with her. It was too bad. Suddenly, I ached for her to stay with me and share more of her strange customs.

Juliette took a bit of the crunchy bread and crumbs cascaded onto her lap and mine. "This is a bit messier than ale."

"Not the way Vandar drink." I brushed some of the crumbs off her lips. She went still, her gaze moving to mine, and her breath hitching in her chest.

My gaze slid to her lips, where a few sugary crumbs still clung. Leaning forward, I kissed them off so softly my skin barely feathered across hers. "You taste as sweet as your breads."

She let out a quiet whimper as I kissed her again, this time parting her lips slightly with my tongue.

When I pulled back, her eyes were half-lidded with desire. "Juliette?"

She scored her fingers through my hair and tugged my head back to hers. "More."

I curled my arm around her waist, flattening her body to mine and making a raw sound as our mouths crashed into each other. Whatever fear or timidness she'd felt before seemed to vanish as she rocked into me, our tongues swirling. She met every stroke of my tongue with an eager one of her own, and the warm sweetness of her mouth made me lightheaded. Need storming through me, and my cock strained against the fabric encircling my waist.

After we'd kissed for so long my lips felt bruised, I pulled away from her, heaving in breaths.

"Is something wrong, Raas?" she asked, her own pink lips puffy.

"I want to taste more of you," I husked. "I want to taste *all* of you."

From the look in her eyes, I could tell she didn't know what I meant, but she nodded. "Yes, Raas."

I flipped her onto her back, hovering over her like a predator, my heart hammering and my cock aching.

CHAPTER TWENTY

Juliette

Had I lost my mind? What was I doing? I'd wanted to make the Raas something as a thank you, but I'd never wanted this. My breath was shallow as he leaned over me, kissing his way down my neck. Or had I?

The feel of his lips, warm and surprisingly soft, had sent desire ricocheting through me, and my skin buzzed as if I'd been shocked. I'd never experienced need slamming into me like this, and as his strong hands caressed me, tugging up the hem of my dress, I was almost powerless to control it.

But I didn't want to control it. I'd spent my entire life doing exactly what was expected of me and obeying the rules of my planet. I'd dressed the right way, and acted the right way, and what had it gotten me? Nothing but loneliness. I arched my back as Vassim closed his mouth around one peaked nipple through the fabric of my dress, sucking it through the cloth and making it harden even more.

I didn't care if I was being foolish or impulsive. All I cared about was how the Raas' touch made me feel alive for the first time. Truly alive and not just going through the motions for the benefit of everyone else.

The blood pounding in my ears was deafening, the sound of the Raas saying my name muffled as he shoved my dress up around my hips, his breath hot on the delicate flesh of my thighs. I'd never been touched by a male before, but my body seemed to know what to do, or at least it knew what it wanted to do. I let my legs fall open, not caring what he might think about me and not caring that he was the first to see my body so exposed.

He lowered his head between my legs, inhaling deeply and growling, the rumble making my body jerk in response.

"You smell so sweet I need to taste you," he said, tugging at my panties.

I was vaguely aware of what he meant. I lifted my head and looked down at him. "You want to kiss me *there?*"

His eyes flashed dark as he peered up at me. "You have never...?"

My cheeks warmed as I shook my head. "Never. I've never done anything."

Another rumble in his chest as he gazed at me. "Do you want this?"

I wasn't entirely sure what "this" entailed, but I wanted it—all of it—whatever it was. "Yes, Raas."

He gave me a wicked grin and pushed me down with one hand. I flopped back, yelping as he then tore off my panties and tossed them aside. Sliding his hands under my ass, he opened me to him, and I instinctively writhed my hips, needing his touch. Then his mouth was on me, his tongue hot as it parted me. I reached down and tangled my fingers in his hair as his tongue did things to me I'd never imagined.

When he found my bundle of nerves, I gasped, almost rearing up off the pallet. He laughed at my reaction, and the vibrations made my eyes roll up into the back of my head. Then he was sucking and flicking me so deftly that I lost all ability to think, wrapping my legs around his shoulders. Every time my body would start to tremble, the Raas would slow his tongue, swirling it languidly until I was panting and begging him for more. Then he would resume his pace, flicking me until I could barely remember to take a breath.

"You want more?" he asked, barely lifting his head.

I bobbed my head up and down frantically, unable to speak.

"Spread your legs wider," he ordered. "Show me how ready you are for me."

When I did, he stared down at me, his expression transfixed. "So perfect and all mine."

Then I felt it, the furry tip of his tail tickling the inside of my thigh as it moved higher. I sucked in a sharp breath when it reached my opening.

The Raas looked up at me as it pushed slowly into me. "You have never heard what Vandar do with our tails?"

I could only stare at where the dark tip of his tail was entering me. Even though it was only his tail, and it was covered in fur, it was still thick and hard underneath. The stretch—and the sight of me taking a Vandar tail—made me tip my head back and moan.

"You're taking my tail so well," he said. "You're almost ready to take my cock."

Then his mouth was on me again, licking my aching bundle of nerves as he moved his tail inside me. It was all too much, and I dug my fingernails into his hair as my body detonated, trembling and moaning as pleasure rippled through me. Vassim didn't stop his tongue's movements until my legs had stopped shaking and my body had sagged.

His tail was still snug inside me, but he was no longer pushing it deeper. Instead, he moved himself up so he was on top of me, with his elbows braced at my side so he wouldn't crush me.

He kissed me lightly. "This time I want to watch you."

"This time?" I managed to say through uneven breaths.

"You didn't think that was all, did you?"

I'd never thought that anything could feel as good as *that* had. I couldn't imagine that there could be more, but if there was more, I wanted it. I wanted everything he could give me.

"Unless you wish me to stop?" he whispered into my ear, as he stroked his tail in and out of me.

"Don't stop," I begged, even though my body was limp with pleasure.

Pulling his head back, he locked his gaze on mine, his eyes dark and molten. He pulled his tail from me, and I immediately missed the way it filled me, letting out a breathy sigh. Before I could tell him that I wanted his tail again, there was something bigger and harder in its place. Something with no fur.

"You felt so good around my tail." He rested his forehead on mine as he pushed into me. "But your tight little body was made to take my cock."

I squirmed from the pressure, his thick crown stretching me much more than his tail had, but he thrust hard, lodging fully inside me. I screamed from the sharp pain as he covered my mouth with kisses, holding himself deep while I adjusted to the size of him. My breaths were ragged, and my hips twitched in a futile effort to escape the intrusion.

"That's a lot bigger than your tail," I said, when I'd regained the ability to speak.

Raas Vassim didn't speak, and I saw that his jaw was clenched, the muscles on the sides trembling.

"Are you okay?"

"You're so tight. I'm fighting the urge to fuck you as hard as I want to."

My heart raced at the thought that I could drive a big, tough Raas to the edge of restraint. The thrill of it was intoxicating. I hooked my legs around his hips. "I want you to fuck me."

He groaned and squeezed his eyes shut. "How can a tiny human like you take me?" He opened his eyes and held mine in an intense gaze. "I don't deserve someone as perfect as you, something as perfect as this." Then he growled low, twitching his head to the side. "But I will take you as mine anyway."

Then he crushed his mouth to mine as he buried his cock in me again and again, his tongue stroking mine with every thrust. Our groans mingled, the sounds swallowed by the slapping of flesh against flesh. The pain gave way to intense pleasure and soon I was rocking my hips up to meet him, wanting to take him deep.

When my body began to tremble, he tore his mouth from mine, never slowing his pace but watching as my release overtook me. This time was faster and harder, my body clenching around his cock and my back arching as I screamed, clawing at his back. With a roar, he pistoned into me, knifing up and pulsing hot before dropping down and tucking his head in my neck as he fought for breath.

I tightened my legs around his waist, not wanting to let him go and lose the intoxicating feeling of being desired and adored, even if it was by an alien warlord I had no business falling for.

CHAPTER TWENTY-ONE

Vassim

Tvek! What had just happened? My arms shook as I braced myself on my elbows so as not to crush her, and I drew in shuddering breaths with my head resting in the crook of her neck.

For a human who'd never been touched before, she'd reacted like no one I'd ever seen. Aside from a few moments of confusion, she'd been almost wild with desire and hadn't held back her moans or her screams. My back even twinged from the bite of her nails across my flesh.

I rolled to one side, flopping on the pallet beside her and staring up at the black ceiling. I'd expected to relish her innocence and shock, but there had been little of that. What I hadn't expected was how right she'd felt. Despite being human—a species that had never impressed me in its battle strategy or physical prowess—she'd held her own against a Vandar. A Raas of the Vandar.

I'd heard tales of weepy virgins too scared to do anything but lie on their backs and close their eyes. But not Juliette. If I hadn't experienced her almost vise-like tightness, I might not have believed she was as innocent as she claimed to be. But her pained scream had been real, as had her shock at me using my tail.

No, she'd been untouched, but surprisingly passionate. And my reaction to her was not what I'd expected. For in as long as I could remember, I'd lost myself in the moment, forgetting my torment as her body had given me sanctuary. Joining with Juliette had been more than fucking. It had been an escape for my body and soul.

Thinking of her cry of pain when I'd entered her, I reached out and pulled her close to me, tucking her head under my chin. "Did I hurt you badly?"

Her head shook. "It wasn't as bad as I expected."

I peered down at her head, golden curls covering most of her face. "You expected being bedded by a Raas of the Vandar would be bad?"

"I meant the pain. It hurt for a moment but then that went away, and it was amazing."

My chest swelled with pride. I'd always enjoyed pleasuring females, even though it had been a while since I'd indulged in a pleasurer. I might like to fuck hard, but there was nothing as arousing as making a female come on my tongue and feeling her writhe with my tail inside her. Not to mention, it got her wet and ready to be ridden hard.

I kissed the top of her head. "I am glad. Being with a Vandar should be nothing short of amazing."

She laughed. "Cocky much?"

I worked the word around in my head. "I do not understand. You have seen my cock. You have had my cock. Is it too much?"

"No." She laughed again. "It's another Earth phrase my sister liked to use. I'm teasing you for being so confident about the Vandar being good in bed. I'm sure not all of you are."

I scoffed at this. "Any raider worth anything knows how to please a female. Besides, we not only have our cocks. We have our tails."

She traced one finger over the marks on my chest. "Do you always use your tails like that?"

"Why?" I put my hand over her meandering finger. "Did you find it unpleasant?"

She hesitated. "No, but I'd never imagined that's what your tails were for."

"That is not the primary purpose for them, but they are the most sensitive part of our bodies, aside from our cocks, so it is pleasurable for us to tail-fuck."

"Tail-fuck?" She almost choked on the word.

I let my hand drift down her back and squeeze her plump ass. "The phrase startles you? Is it too…cocky?"

She giggled. "No, but you should probably stick to the universal tongue and Vandar. Twenty-first century Earth slang sounds a bit funny coming from you."

"Why does your sister like it so much?" I asked. I'd only laid eyes on her older sister once and never spoken to her, but the human that Corvak took as a mate had struck me as a very different creature than Juliette. Where Juliette was all delicious curves and golden curls, her sister had been lanky and athletic with her hair pulled back tightly, a fitting match for the former battle chief who'd been exiled.

If I thought about it, my attraction to such a soft, feminine human made no sense. As a fierce Raas of the Vandar, I should want a mate like Juliette's sister—a female equally tough and battle-ready. But I didn't. I craved the sensual curves and shy smiles of Juliette. She felt like the right match for me—the light to my dark and the soft to my hard.

"I don't exactly know," Juliette said. "Maybe she wanted to preserve something of the planet we came from, even though we never saw it. Maybe it was her way of being rebellious, since the natives on our planet didn't understand her retro phrases."

"Your sister liked being rebellious?"

"Sienna?" She let out a throaty laugh that was nothing like her usual giggles. "It was like oxygen to her. If she wasn't pushing back against something, I doubt she'd have been happy. Not that she was ever happy on Kimithion III."

"Were you?"

Her hand twitched under my own. "I thought I was, but now I realize that I was going through the motions and trying to make everyone else happy. The only thing I had that was truly mine and that brought me joy was baking."

I growled and gave her ass cheek another squeeze. "Your baking has also brought me joy." I was glad to change the subject from her sister. Guilt gnawed at me, since I could have told the bounty hunters that Juliette was on my ship, but I had not. And now that they'd gone dark because of their mission, I could not.

Juliette wiggled as if trying to escape my grasp, but her attempts were not genuine. "Me baking for you wasn't supposed to end up like this."

"No? But I enjoyed your thank you very much." I pulled her closer. "I might have to give you a hundred Gerwyns."

"Don't do that! Furb is cute, but one is plenty, thank you."

"Just one? Does that mean you don't wish to repeat this?" Even though my voice was teasing, my question was sincere. I didn't want to get my hopes up, if Juliette regretted what we'd done.

She pushed herself up to sitting. "I didn't say that, but is it okay if we don't do it right away?"

"You're sore?"

She glanced down, her expression stricken. "That, and I'm making a mess of your mattresses." Her eyes grew wide. "Is it normal for me to be leaking?"

"It is when I fill you with my seed."

Her face didn't change. "Seed?"

Just how innocent was she? I sat up and stole a quick glance at her sticky thighs, tinged with a faint hint of blood. "The blood is because it was your first time, but the rest is from me. Did no one tell you that when males fuck, they fill you with seed?"

Her gaze dropped, and she shook her head. "No one ever mentioned anything wet and sticky."

An urge to shelter and protect Juliette surged through me. It was as if my seed had indeed marked her as mine and mine alone. I fought back the compulsion to bury my cock inside her and fill her again, my hot pulses branding her as mine.

Instead, I scooped her up and headed for the bathing pools. "It is nothing that can't be washed off. And you don't need to fear becoming with child. That can only happen if we were mates, and you carried my mating marks."

She reflexively touched a hand to the mound of her belly. "Child?"

"Like I said, it is nothing to worry about. A Vandar can only impregnate his true mate, and that can only happen with mating marks." My heart squeezed with the sudden desire to see my marks swirling across her pristine skin. "For now, you are safe."

What I told her was true, but I suspected very strongly that *I* was no longer safe. I stepped into the tepid green water, walking deep enough that we were both enveloped by the murky water.

She unwound her arms from my neck. "So I won't get mating marks just because we…?"

"If marks appeared on every female we fucked, the entire galaxy might be covered in Vandar marks," I said, then instantly regretted my words.

Before I could say more, there was a pounding on the outside door.

CHAPTER TWENTY-TWO

Vassim

"Report!" I stomped onto the command deck, the ends of my hair still damp against my bare back. I'd leapt out of the bathing pool when the pounding had not ceased, answering the door in nothing but the crumpled fabric I'd snatched from the sleeping pallets and thrown around my waist. The warrior who'd told me I was needed urgently on the command deck hadn't seemed startled by my lack of clothing, or the water dripping around my feet. My only regret was that I hadn't had time to explain much to Juliette before I was tugging on my boots and battle kilt and bolting out the door.

"A priority distress call, Raas." Taan twisted from where he stood at a sleek black console. "From Carlogia Prime."

My heart still raced from my run through the ship, and I strode to the platform overlooking the rest of the consoles and warriors manning the command deck, leaning forward and gripping the metal railing. "I know that name. Why do I know the name of that planet?'

"It was recently liberated from the empire by the hordes of Raas Kratos and Raas Kaalek."

That was it. The Vandar victory there had resulted in many lost imperial soldiers and ships. "And now they send out a distress call?"

Taan tapped his fingers across the screen of his console and static filled the room. The transmission was weak and the signal spotty, but the voice that came through was clearly in distress.

"Transmitting on an encrypted Vandar channel to any Vandar horde within range. This is Fenrey of Carlogia Prime. Zagrath ships have appeared over Carlogia again, and we fear they intend to resume their mining operations. You said to use this channel if we ever needed help again." There was a heavy pause. "We need your help, Vandar raiders."

Then the voice disappeared, and there was only the hiss of static. All the warriors stood motionless at their posts for a moment before Taan discontinued the transmission.

"This Carlogian mentioned mining," I said. "Tell me about the planet."

Taan swiped his screen. "Pre-warp society, with a developed societal structure. Their core contains rare minerals that the empire previously mined for use in their technology and weapons. Our last raiding mission on the imperial cargo ship brought us closer to Carlogia Prime. We could be there within a single standard rotation."

I clenched my hands around the metal rail until my knuckles went white. "Our hordes repelled them, but now they have returned? We'll see about that." I cut my eyes to the battle chief station that remained empty, then looked away just as quickly.

"You wish to engage, Raas?" My *majak* joined me on the platform.

"Where are the other hordes? The ones who are familiar with Carlogia Prime?"

"Too far out of range to receive the transmission. Or, at least to receive it in time to respond. Raas Bron, who took over Raas Kratos' horde, is no longer in this sector, and the last reports of Raas Kaalek have him nearing Zagrath headquarters."

I nodded. That sounded like Raas Kaalek—running headlong into the mouth of the beast. It also put him too far away to reach the threatened alien planet before the empire seized control.

"It looks like we'll be going this alone," I said. Although I intended to send an encrypted message to the bounty hunters, they'd gone dark and might not receive it or be able to respond.

A rumble of approval passed through the warriors on deck. Alone was how we'd battled in the far reaches of space where the rules of war were easily discarded, as were the rules of law. My warriors preferred it that way, as did I.

"Set a course for the planet and alert the rest of the horde about our intentions," I told Taan. "And hail the bounty hunters." I lifted a fist into the air and raised my voice to a boom. "Prepare the ship for battle!"

Fists pumped high as low bellows joined my own. Heavy boots stomped the floor, making it shake.

My *majak* returned to his console, his fingers flying as he sent transmissions. "The bounty hunter ship has responded to hails, Raas."

"Onscreen," I ordered, facing forward and clasping my hands behind my back.

Once again, the Dothvek warrior K'alvek appeared on our view screen, his gold skin a sharp contrast to the Vandar standing next to him.

"K'alvek." I inclined my head at him, acknowledging him as the leader of the ship. "Corvak."

Both men nodded at me, but it was the former Vandar battle chief who spoke. "Raas Vassim." He clicked his heels together, the movement and sound barely noticeable since I only saw the warriors from the waist up. Still, I valued the gesture of respect. "We were surprised to be hailed by you so soon. We have been following your raiding missions." His lips curled into a smile. "The empire is very displeased by your relentless attacks."

I returned his smile. "I am glad to hear it. The empire has earned every moment of its fate."

"Do you require assistance?" K'alvek asked.

"It is not we who require assistance. We have intercepted a distress call from the planet of Carlogia Prime." I nodded to Taan, who played the transmission for the bounty hunters.

When it was over, both males were frowning.

"You have been to this planet, yes?" I asked.

"We both have," Corvak answered. "It is how we met."

K'alvek nodded beside him. "We were chasing a bounty we believed to be Raas Kaalek."

"The bounty the empire had set was actually on Raas Kratos," Corvak added. "While the bounty hunters were on the planet, having tracked Raas Kaalek and his human mate to the surface where they'd crashed, Raas Kratos joined with his brother's horde to liberate the planet and retrieve the Raas."

I exchanged a look with my *majak* then turned back to the screen. "Things with the Raas brothers sound complicated."

Corvak grunted. "They could be. As much as they did not get along as boys, they are still brothers."

"Do you believe the Raas brothers will answer the hail from Carlogia Prime?" I asked.

"Raas Kaalek owes his life to the Carlogians. He will not hesitate. I would say the same about Raas Kratos, only because the planet harbored his brother and he is grateful to them for that, but he is no longer Raas."

"And Raas Bron?" I didn't know everything about the former battle chief's history with the new Raas, but Bron had exiled him and stripped him of his beloved position in the horde.

Corvak's jaw tightened as he thought. Finally, he loosed a breath. "Raas Bron is an honorable Vandar. He will answer the call."

I nodded, impressed that Corvak had put any personal feelings aside to assess his former Raas. It spoke to his own honor. "That may be so, but neither will reach the planet before us. Can we count on your assistance to once again fight off the empire's overreach?"

"You do not need to ask," K'alvek said. "My crew also holds fond memories of the Carlogians. We do not wish to see them suffer. We will set a course for the planet now and gladly join you in battle."

He swiveled and gave orders to the dark-haired female pilot behind him who waved cheerily from her seated console. I was reminded of their mixed crew of males and females, humans, Dothveks, Zevrians, and shape-shifters. Even with this knowledge, I was startled when a female appeared beside Corvak.

Although her hair was honey-brown and not gold, and it was pulled up into a high knot on her head, I could immediately discern the subtle similarities between Juliette and her sister. My stomach clenched as I recognized the plump lips they shared—the same lips I'd so eagerly kissed—and the shape of their eyes, even if Corvak's mate's eyes were not blue.

This was Sienna, the sister Juliette had told me about, and the mate that had provoked Corvak to fly with the bounty hunters instead of with my horde. As she peered at me through the screen, I could see the shrewdness that her sister did not possess. The thought of Juliette waiting for me in my quarters made me look away from Sienna.

I could tell Sienna that her sister was safe with me. But that would bring about a slew of questions I was not prepared to answer—how she got on board my ship, why I did not return her to her planet, why she remained in my quarters. No doubt, it would also prompt a request for Juliette to be reunited to Sienna. They were sisters, after all, and as Corvak had reminded me when he spoke of the Raas brothers, family could fight, but they were always family.

I was not prepared to release Juliette. Not yet. I thought about the sensation of being inside her and how enthusiastically she'd responded to me. How perfect she'd felt. How whole and undamaged she'd made me feel. Maybe not ever.

I cleared my throat and focused on the two males on the screen. "We look forward to joining you in battle."

CHAPTER TWENTY-THREE

Juliette

Furb scampered around the edge of the pool, dipping his nose in the water, yipping, and then scuttling away.

"I don't get it, either." I rested my arms on the stone ledge and my chin on top of my folded hands. The Raas had run off so quickly that I hadn't been able to get a better explanation from him. If what we'd just done didn't produce mating marks, what did?

I shivered as I tried to imagine what other things the alien might be able to do with his tail. As much as I'd liked everything he'd done to me, I couldn't help the flush that warmed my cheeks. Even the whispers I'd heard about males back on my home world hadn't covered anything like *this*.

The fluffy Gerwyn ran up again, rubbing against my face and emitting a strange rumbling sound that vibrated his body. I patted him lazily before he ran back out to the bedroom, no doubt to curl up on a pillow and doze off. Gerwyns did seem to sleep a lot.

I let my legs float up behind me, swishing them through the water. The stickiness was gone, but the ache between my legs remained. I squeezed them together. It wasn't a bad ache, though, and I liked the memory it provoked—of Raas Vassim working himself thickly between my legs while his warm breath mingled with mine.

Despite my self-conscious blush, for the first time in my life I felt a rush of power. I'd been the one to make the Raas throw his head back and roar, the muscles on his neck strained as he'd quivered and finally sagged on top of me. I might not have known exactly what I was doing, but my body had instinctively taken over, and my moans and movements had been impossible to rein in, even if I'd wanted to.

"Snap out of it," I scolded myself, using another of Sienna's favorite phrases. "Like the Raas said, it was only fucking, and he's done it with tons of females."

That thought bothered me, although I was fully aware that the Vandar species didn't have the same morality rules that I'd grown up with in Kimithion III. They viewed sex and nudity as something completely normal and natural, and nothing to be secretive about or feel shame for. The Vandar openly visited pleasure planets and enjoyed sex that they paid for, whereas that wasn't even heard of on my home world. Again, thinking of Raas Vassim with a pleasurer made me frown, especially when I realized that they'd all been more experienced than me. But I could hardly get jealous over a Raas I had no intention of staying with, no matter how much I enjoyed the things he'd done to me. Besides, I thought, I did not want to get mating marks, so it was good that I couldn't get them from being fucked by the Raas.

"Because I definitely want to do that again," I whispered to myself, smiling at my own naughtiness. I might not be staying with the Raas, but there was nothing that said I couldn't enjoy my time before the two moons aligned and he had to return me to Kimithion III.

Thinking of my home world wiped all the warm, steamy thoughts from my mind. Did I really want to go back home? What was waiting for me? My drunk father who might not even have noticed I was gone—that is, until he got hungry. My sister was gone and would probably never return, not that I blamed her. There was nothing left for Sienna there. Was there anything left for me?

I'd always expected to marry some man and have a family while continuing with my baking. It had never been a thrilling future, but it had seemed steady and solid—something to look forward to when things at home had been depressing. But could that even happen now? I was no longer pure, and any man who married me would get a shock if he expected me to be. Once word got out that I'd been held by the Vandar, rumors would swirl that I'd been bedded by them. Rumors that wouldn't be untrue. I tried to bring up the face of an eligible mate on Kimithion III, but they all faded away, dull and forgettable, compared to Raas Vassim with his wild black hair and his swishing tail.

Then I forced myself to envision a life on the Vandar warbird. Even though it was completely different from what I'd been used to—the cold darkness a shock after living on an arid, sunlit planet—it was not without its luxuries. Take the bathing pools. I scissored my legs through the water again, the soreness already fading from the minerals within. There was nothing like this at home. Not to mention the large quarters that I didn't have to share with my drunk father. There was only the Raas to share the expansive pallets, and he definitely fell in the plus column. There was no man who came close to Raas Vassim.

Even as I became aware of my shifting feelings toward leaving the horde and Vassim, there was a niggling voice in the back of my head reminding me that the only reason the Raas had kept me and desired me to stay was because I had the potential to break his curse. Without that, would he have given me a second glance?

I was pretty sure he couldn't have faked his arousal in bed, but I didn't know enough to know if that was the way he was with every female he'd bedded. I'd felt a powerful connection to him, but for him it could have been just like with all the others. That thought made a cold ball harden in my gut.

"It doesn't matter," I said, under my breath. "None of this matters, if you don't get mating marks and break the curse. He's promised to take you home, and if the curse remains on him, that's what he'll do. It won't matter how much you're falling for him, or that you'll have no life back on Kimithion III. A Vandar Raas won't break his promise."

I swallowed hard, the reality of returning home and leaving Vassim making my throat thick. After all my begging to go home, was I actually wishing I could stay?

"Come on, girl. The sex wasn't that amazing."

But it was, and Raas Vassim was. I couldn't deny that he fascinated me and provoked feelings in me that I'd never experienced before. When I was with him, I was no longer timid Juliette, taking care of everyone around her. I was someone bolder. My face flamed. I was someone who's been fucked by a Vandar tail and had loved it. I dunked my head all the way under the water, hoping to douse my burning cheeks and cool myself off. Thinking of Vassim's tail inside me was doing nothing for that.

"You're in so much trouble," I said to myself, once I'd popped out of the water and dragged my hands down my wet hair.

"Have you committed a crime since I've been away?'

I opened my eyes, startled to see the Raas standing in the doorway.

"When did you…? I thought you were… Is everything okay?"

He eyed me with a dark, predatory gaze, shedding his clothes quickly and leaving them in a pile as he crossed the black, glossy floor and dropped into the water behind me.

Before I could turn to face him, he'd pressed his large body against mine, his heat only enflaming me further. "Everything is fine now."

I gripped the stone ledge as he spread my legs with his knee then dragged the crown of his cock through my folds, the water making me even more slippery. "I thought you were needed for a raiding mission, or something."

He lowered his head beside mine and nipped my ear. "We're en route to a battle, but there is nowhere more important for me to be than here." He notched his cock at my opening, tilting my hips up with one hand, and thrusting hard. He moaned as I sucked in a desperate breath at the familiar stretch. "Inside you."

I leaned my head back, savoring the sensation of being filled completely by the alien warlord and letting all my doubts melt away as he stroked into me.

CHAPTER TWENTY-FOUR

Vassim

The iron walkway rocked from side to side as I leapt off it onto a platform, clutching a beam overhead as the warbird pitched to one side.

Tvek. I righted myself and continued racing toward the command deck, cursing at myself for staying too long with Juliette. Not that I regretted a moment I'd spent buried inside her, the water splashing over the stone ledge of the bathing pools and spilling across the shiny floor. I'd taken her from behind, curling one hand around her waist to pleasure her with my hand while I pounded into her. After she'd come and screamed my name, I'd flipped her around and held her with her legs wrapped around my waist, moving her up and down on my cock until I'd no longer been able to hold back, exploding with a euphoric fury that had almost brought me to my knees.

Even now, as the ship shuddered from incoming weapons fire, my cock stirred as I thought about the sounds of water sloshing onto the floor and our moans echoing off the glossy stone. I groaned and pushed my cock down with one hand. Fucking her was a much better way to stay awake than wandering the dark corridors of the ship deranged from lack of sleep, but although I was more refreshed than usual, I had a hard time getting thoughts of her out of my mind. I needed to forget about the female in my quarters and focus on my horde and my ship, before we were all blown out of the sky.

I took a wide set of stairs two at a time, hoisting myself up and bursting onto the command deck. "What the *tvek* is happening?"

Taan held the sides of his console with both hands to keep from being knocked off his feet, craning his neck to look back at me. "We've arrived at Carlogia Prime, Raas."

I looked at the wide view screen and the planet, fronted by what looked like a fleet of imperial battleships, dull-gray and hulking like square-shouldered sentries. "Along with half the empire."

"It was a trap, Raas." Taan gripped the console so tightly, I could see the white of his bones. "When we reached Carlogia Prime and fired a warning shot across the bow of the single Zagrath ship orbiting the planet, these ships appeared from behind a moon."

"The Carlogians set us up?"

Taan shook his head. "Doubtful. I suspect they were unaware of the fleet hidden behind the moon. The ships didn't appear on our sensors until we fired."

I clenched my teeth. "Not a bad ruse. Sometimes I forget that not all the Zagrath are fools."

"We're trying to retreat but the horde ships have been divided by the fleet, so we can't use the amoeba defense or attack pattern. And because there are so many battleships, they're able to fire indiscriminately."

Another blast rocked me almost off my feet. "So these are lucky hits?"

"They pegged our location when we fired, but we've since moved position so they are firing blind."

"But still hitting us." I growled at the damage we were taking and the fact that we'd been outsmarted by our enemy. But most of all, I was angry at myself for being distracted and away from the command deck when we'd reached the planet.

I stomped over to the platform and braced my arms on the railing, berating myself for my weakness. I was not some fresh-faced apprentice who'd never been with a female before. I was a Raas of the Vandar—battle-scarred, ruthless, unrelenting. I should not allow one female, no matter how alluring, to distract me from my mission. But Juliette… Again, my pulse quickened, not from the battle, but from thoughts of her.

"Any word from the bounty hunter ship?" I asked, my gaze fixed on the imperial ships and the red laser fire firing from the dark underbellies of their massive battleships.

"Nothing, Raas," my *majak* said, staggering over to stand next to me and grabbing the rail to stay upright. "They were always going to arrive after us."

I glanced over my shoulder at a communications officer. "Send a message on an encrypted channel to the bounty hunters. Warn them of the ambush."

"Should I tell them not to come?" he asked, his fingers dancing across the dark surface of his console.

"Don't bother. Corvak would come no matter what we said."

He gave a single nod and returned his focus on his screen.

When I turned back, lowered my voice so only my *majak* could hear. "Have the female taken from my quarters to the hangar bay. I want her ready to escape if this does not work."

Taan gave me a sharp nod. "What is *this*, Raas?"

I squared my shoulders, with my legs set wide. "We need to get on the outside of the ring of imperial ships."

"They've surrounded us with laser fire," Taan said. "The only way out is through, and we'll most likely sustain more damage than we can withstand."

I studied the arrangement of the ships and the pattern of their firing. "Because they're working off the assumption we're inside their blockade."

Taan furrowed his brow. "We are."

"But we're using our invisibility shielding. They can't know that for sure." I hurried over to the communications console, nudging the officer out of the way. "This might not work, but it's worth a try."

While my *majak* returned to his console, ordering Juliette to be escorted from my quarters, I sent a message in Vandar on one of the internal encrypted channels used by our network of horde ships. Holding my breath, I peered at the viewscreen and waited. I wasn't disappointed. Soon, concentrated Vandar weapons fire appeared on the far side of the battleships, arching through the air and pounding the enemy ships.

Taan gaped at the screen. "It looks like it's coming from a large ship—a lead ship."

"Our ship," I said, pointing to a pilot. "Now that they're distracted and think they're being attacked by the lead horde ship from behind, get us the *tvek* out of here."

"Yes, Raas."

The ship pivoted away from the battleships, skirting the smaller ships behind us and deftly flying through the ring of imperial vessels. Once we were outside the line of fire, I sent another message to the horde ships, ordering them to disperse and regroup with us for the amoeba attack formation.

I returned to the platform and Taan rejoined me. "Now we can show the empire what happens when they try to trick the Vandar."

Taan shook his head, giving me a grin. "Just when I think you can't surprise me anymore, Raas."

"This should hold them off until the bounty hunters arrive, or any other hordes that might have intercepted the distress call."

"No need," one of the tactical officers called over the beeping consoles and loud voices. "Another ship just dropped into orbit."

"The bounty hunters?" I asked.

"Affirmative. But they aren't alone."

CHAPTER TWENTY-FIVE

Juliette

"What do you mean *leave?*" I stared at the Neebix apprentice as he stood in the arch of the doorway.

The ship shook, and Baru twirled the fur of his tail around one finger. "Orders from the Raas. You're to be taken to the hangar bay in case we need to get you to an escape shuttle before the ship blows up."

"Blows up?" Fear iced my skin, the remaining droplets of water on my wet flesh chilling me to the bone. I glanced down at the gauzy dress I'd found in the back of a drawer, a pale-green swirl of fabric that I'd assumed was left by the pleasurer Baru had mentioned. I'd thought it was pretty, but the thought of wearing it to escape during a space battle now seemed absurd.

"That probably won't happen, but the Raas doesn't want to put you at risk." He waved for me to follow him. "Come on."

I scanned the room, spotted the yellow puff that was Furb, and ran to scoop him up. He yipped in protest, his soft fur fluffing up and his spiky tail twitching, but I patted him on the head. "Don't worry, buddy. It's going to be okay."

"You're bringing that?" Baru eyed the Gerwyn as if *it* might explode.

I clutched Furb closer. "Of course, I am."

Baru shrugged, clearly thinking my attachment to the creature was strange. "You have nothing else?"

I shook my head, not bothering to glance behind me again. Once we'd left the room and walked down the corridor a little way, I stopped. "What about the Raas? Will he be coming with me?"

Baru barely cut his eyes to me. "The Raas stays with the ship."

"Even if the ship is going to be destroyed?"

"Especially then. No Raas would abandon his warriors to die alone."

My gut clenched. I'd never have imagined that I could feel so sick at the thought of a Vandar warlord dying with his ship, especially one who'd taken me captive, but things had changed. He wasn't just a battle-hardened raider who loomed dark and terrifying in my dreams. He was a tortured soul who was loyal, brave, and on occasions, tender. And he was mine.

"I'm not leaving without the Raas."

Baru spun on his heel to face me, the horns buried in his curly hair flushing pink. "What?"

I stood my ground. "You heard me. If the Raas is staying, then so am I."

Baru muttered something about never being made a raider and being put out an airlock as he grabbed the tip of his tail and worked it between his hands. "You were quiet and scared. Everyone said so. That's why they gave you to me. You were supposed to be easy."

I had been quiet and scared when I'd arrived. Maybe it was being with the Raas, or maybe it was something in the air on the Vandar warbird, but I didn't feel like the timid creature who'd fainted that first day. That version of me seemed far away and foreign.

"The Raas will kill me if anything happens to you," Baru mumbled, more to himself than to me. "I'm in charge of getting you to safety. If I fail…" He made a squeaking noise, his horns now flaming red.

The last thing I wanted to do was get the apprentice in trouble after he'd been so nice to me, and he seemed genuinely petrified about what would happen to him if he failed. I didn't want to tell him that if I blew up with the ship, he would too, so he shouldn't worry about it. That seemed unusually harsh. The ship trembled with another hit, and a siren wailed overhead.

"Listen." I put a hand on his arm. "I'll go with you, but I need to see the Raas first."

He frowned. "He's busy on the command deck. I can't take you there."

"We could go back to his quarters."

He huffed out a resigned breath. "Fine, I will take you to the command deck, but I'm telling you this isn't a good idea. You've never seen the Raas when he's in full battle mode."

My stomach flipped nervously, but I steeled myself. "I can handle the Raas."

Baru muttered darkly under his breath, and I wondered if I was making a big mistake. Saying I could handle the Raas was a pretty big exaggeration. I hadn't known him for long, and even though he'd shown me other sides of him, the Neebix apprentice was right. I hadn't seen him in all situations, and I didn't know what he was like when he was focused on battle and being the Raas.

I shook off my doubts as Baru led me up through the ship, raiders thundering by us as the ship continued to take weapons fire. They barely gave me a sideways glance as they pounded down iron stairs and yelled Vandar war chants. The hairs on the back of my neck stood up as the war cries echoed through the cavernous warbird, the booming voices rattling my bones.

I would feel better once I saw Vassim, I told myself. If I could just talk to him, the fear clawing its way up my throat would vanish. Despite the obvious fact that the ship was under attack, I'd never seen a warrior as fierce as Raas Vassim, and I had faith that he could defeat anything.

Baru stopped at the top of a long staircase, and I leaned against one of the rails to catch my breath. There was nothing easy about traversing the inside of a Vandar warbird.

"The command deck is through here," he said, inclining his head toward massive steel double doors, "but it's probably going to be chaotic, so we need to slip in the back and wait until the Raas can be interrupted."

My pulse fluttered, both nervous at what lay beyond the doors and thrilled to see the Raas again. "Understood."

Baru stepped forward and the doors slid open. I had no idea if they moved silently or not because the command deck bustled with noise and activity. Like the rest of the Vandar ship, the light was low and iron beams were exposed overhead. Bare-chested raiders in battle kilts stood at dark standing consoles as a siren continued to wail. Machines beeped and warriors called out to each other over the buzz of static in the background. Stretching across the entire width of the far wall was a screen that showed the battle taking place, hulking gray vessels firing red toward us.

Baru tugged me forward and over to one side of the door. No one noticed our arrival, certainly not Raas Vassim who stood on a raised platform with his first officer. My heart raced at the sight of his broad, muscular back and his hands clasped behind him.

"On screen," he commanded.

The view of space disappeared, and in its place was a face I recognized. Corvak. The Vandar raider who'd been exiled to my planet and had fallen for my sister.

I gasped, but the sound was swallowed up by the commotion around me.

"Looks like the empire brought its big guns," Corvak said.

The Raas unclenched his hands and leaned forward. "It was a trap. We just escaped their net."

"Looks like we arrived in time then." Corvak frowned. "How much damage did your horde sustain?"

"Not enough to hobble us, but we are glad of your arrival. When we last spoke, I did not think you would get here as quickly as you did."

Corvak bowed his head slightly. "I will always answer the call of the Vandar."

My breath caught in my throat. Raas Vassim had been in communication with Corvak? He'd known where my sister was, and he'd never told me—or her?

"Who did you bring with you?" Raas Vassim asked.

"Our pilot used to fly for the Valox resistance. She put out a call, and they also answered." Corvak's mouth twitched into a half grin. "There is plenty of hatred of the empire to go around."

"We welcome all warriors. This might have been a trap to lure us here, but Carlogia Prime is still in danger. We've picked up imperial vessels on the planet's surface."

"We will go down to the planet, since our ship is more maneuverable."

The Raas nodded. "I will send transports to join you."

Corvak's smile faded as his gaze drifted over the Raas' head and landed on me. "Before we finish devising our battle plan, Raas, maybe you should explain why my mate's sister is standing behind you."

Raas Vassim and his first officer spun around, both of their mouths going slack when they saw me. A Vandar curse escaped Baru's lips as the Raas' gaped at me.

I was too angry to say anything to Vassim, and I no longer cared about speaking with him. Tears blurred my vision, making Corvak's enormous, shocked face a haze on the screen. Raas Vassim had been in contact with the bounty hunter ship my sister was on, and had never bothered to mention it to me, or let me see her. All the tenderness I'd felt for him shattered, replaced by the familiar ache to see my sister.

But at the moment, all I wanted to do was get off the ship and away from the Vandar who'd been hiding the truth from me. I tightened my grip on the squirming Furb in my arms and ran off the command deck.

CHAPTER TWENTY-SIX

Vassim

Even amidst the noises and chaos of the battle, the universe went still as I met Juliette's gaze across the command deck. I had barely registered my shock that she was there before I was leveled by her look of betrayal. Then she turned and ran away, disappearing through the doors with her green dress fluttering behind her. The Neebix boy ran after her after shooting me a look that was both apologetic and confused.

"Raas!" Taan's voice jerked me back to reality.

My heart hammered wildly as the sounds of the battle and my warriors rushed back to me. I pivoted back to the screen. "I do not have time to elaborate on her presence here, but she was not taken from her planet. She snuck aboard my ship."

Corvak's brows shot up in obvious disbelief. "Sienna's younger sister snuck onto a Vandar warbird? On purpose?"

I did not want to answer that question, so I didn't. "I promise you she is not being held against her will."

He didn't look convinced, and he glanced furtively over his shoulder. "My mate will insist on seeing her."

A possessive urge overtook me. As foolish as it was, I did not want to share Juliette, even with her sister. But I bit back the harsh refusal that almost tripped from my tongue. "First we must concentrate on defeating the Zagrath and saving Carlogia Prime."

Corvak frowned. "Agreed. Then we will discuss the human female on your ship and her safe return to her family."

I bristled at the cushioned rebuke and near-command from the Vandar, then reminded myself that Juliette was his mate's sister, which made him her family. He was only behaving as a male family member would when defending a sister. He was actually showing restraint, perhaps because I was a Raas, or perhaps because I was called the *Lunori* Raas.

Taan cleared his throat. "We should provide cover for the bounty hunter ship as it descends to the planet, Raas."

"Yes." I squeezed my hands together behind my back to steady myself, regaining my equilibrium as I focused on the battle strategy. I locked my gaze on Corvak. "We will send ships down with you to fight off any attacks, and provide air cover from our horde ships."

"The Valox fighters will aid you in taking out the enemy battleships," Corvak said, his voice also resuming its usual tone. "They are well-versed at fighting the Zagrath. Between your amoeba attack formation and their assistance, you should be well-matched."

"Let us hope we can repel the empire for good this time."

With a final grunt, Corvak vanished from the screen, and Taan moved off to his own console to implement the plan we'd just devised. I stood for a beat to absorb what had happened. How had Juliette ended up on my command deck when I'd ordered her to an escape shuttle? I wanted to blame the apprentice, but he looked as distraught as anyone. No, Juliette must have insisted on coming.

My heart squeezed as I contemplated her reasons. Did she not want to leave without me? Had she felt compelled to see me before getting on an escape pod? The smallest amount of hope fluttered in my chest and then crumpled to ash as I remembered the pained expression on her face before she'd run away. Whatever feelings she'd had for me had been destroyed once she'd seen Corvak, because then she'd known that I'd been able to contact her sister…and hadn't.

It didn't matter that we'd made a deal for her to stay with me, or that she'd snuck on my ship in the first place. I knew she'd been running away to find her sister, and I'd intentionally kept Juliette from her. I'd wanted to keep her with me for as long as possible, even if it meant hiding the truth from her. If she'd gotten my mating marks and broken my curse, it would have been worth it. But she had no marks, and now she knew I'd been keeping her sister's location from her.

"You have the command," I told Taan as I strode toward the door.

"Raas!" He hurried after me, grasping my arm outside the door. "I know you are concerned that the human saw Corvak, but…"

"You don't understand, *majak*."

His gaze bored into me. "I understand that you are Raas, and we are in the middle of a battle. You can find her once we've defeated the empire."

I shook off his grip. "It cannot wait. You are my most trusted officer. You know what to do."

"Vassim." His use of my name alone stopped me. "No one cherishes females more than me, but we are Vandar raiders. We do not let females rule us."

"This is not just any female, *majak*," I said, the certainly of my words settling over me. "Juliette is mine. I will not lose her, and I will not give her up."

He gave me a pained look. "You still believe she will break the curse?"

"I don't care about the curse." I backed away from him. "All I care about is her."

I didn't glance back as I leapt down the stairs, landing with a thud that rattled the metal floor. I rushed through the ship toward the hangar bay, pushing past the steady flow of raiders running to battle posts or with me to the hangar bay.

I took only a moment to duck my head inside my quarters. As I expected, she was not there. No, she'd been too upset to return to wait for me. If I was correct, she would try to get off the ship in any way possible. Since she'd already stowed aboard a vessel once, I didn't put it past her to try to sneak on another one. I only hoped the Neebix apprentice would slow her down or keep her from leaving.

For the first time, I regretted not posting Vandar guards outside the doors of my quarters. At first, I hadn't deemed it necessary because she was too terrified to wander the warbird by herself, and later I didn't bother because I thought she was content to stay on the ship and with me. For a brief time, I'd even thought she was happy. My mind returned to my body cocooning hers in the bathing pool, one hand cupping her full breast and another swirling around her slick little nub. Her moans of pleasure had been as real as mine. I pressed my lips together to stifle a roar of frustration.

I could not lose her. Not when I'd finally found someone who soothed my tumultuous soul and made me feel whole. Not when I'd found my one true mate. The realization was a jolt that almost sent me stumbling across a suspended walkway. I caught myself before I went spiraling over the side, gripping the steel railing and sucking in a breath.

Juliette was my one true mate. I didn't need mating marks to tell me. I'd never been so consumed by a female before, and I'd had plenty of females tempt me. But none had been such a balm to my heart, and none had made my torment seem so insignificant. It made no sense that a Raas of the Vandar would find his match in a tiny, human female—and one who was the furthest thing from a warrior—but I didn't care. I also didn't care whether she broke the curse or not. She'd already broken the curse of my hardened heart, and that was enough.

I ran the rest of the way without pausing, bursting into the hangar bay and scanning the bustling space. I saw no hint of her pale green dress or of the Neebix apprentice. Only broad chested raiders gripping battle axes as they boarded shiny, black transport ships. Several clicked their heels when they saw me.

"Raas," one of the hangar bay engineers approached me holding a tablet. "We are sending ships with the bounty hunter vessel as you requested."

"How many have already departed?"

He tilted his head at me. "Three. Do you wish to join one of the transports to the surface?"

"Tell me, Vandar. Did the human female get into one of the ships?"

His eyes widened. "No, Raas. We would not send the female on a ship of battle."

Relief surged through me, then I hesitated. "But was she here?"

"She was, with the Neebix and that little Gerwyn." He shuddered at the mention of the spiky-tailed creature. "But I told her she would have to wait until the battle ships had departed before I could send her on an escape shuttle." He glanced around as if just remembering this. "She should be waiting around here somewhere."

If I was correct, Juliette was *not* waiting. She'd snuck onto a ship already, and was headed to the surface of Carlogia Prime to meet the bounty hunter ship and reunite with her sister.

I growled and strode toward one of loading transports. "Your Raas will be joining you on the planet."

Cheers went up among the raiders as fists were thrust into the air. I jumped onto the nearest transport, grabbing an overhead bar to keep me steady. "For Vandar!"

My raiders joined in my war cry. "For Vandar!"

The ramp to the transport lifted and slammed shut, the engines roaring as we tore across the floor of the hangar bay and into space. I rested my free hand on the hilt of my battle axe, my heart pounding. My mate would not escape me so easily.

CHAPTER TWENTY-SEVEN

Juliette

"I'm never going to be made a raider," Baru whispered. "Not after this."

"Shhh." I put a finger to my lips as we huddled in the dark storage area. The transport ship was considerably smaller than the ship I'd originally stowed away on, and the storage unit barely held me, the Neebix boy, and Furb. "I told you that you didn't need to come."

"If I let you sneak off to Carlogia Prime alone, I'd be put out an airlock." He sighed in the dark. "At least this way, I can make sure you don't do anything else foolish."

"I told you, I'm going to the planet to find my sister. It's not foolish."

"Leaving the Raas without permission is a bad idea."

I didn't reply. He was right. I shouldn't be running away from Raas Vassim, but I couldn't bear looking at him after I'd discovered his betrayal. Even thinking about it now made my throat thick. How could he have been in communication with the bounty hunter ship and not told me? He knew how much I wanted to see my sister, and he'd kept her from me.

Did he think I would have gone back on my agreement with him? I would have been happy just seeing her on the view screen like I'd seen Corvak. But was that true? Even as I thought the words, I knew they were lies. Even if I'd agreed to stay and fulfill my promise, Sienna never would have allowed it.

She would have insisted I be returned to her and probably would have hijacked the bounty hunter ship and flown after the Vandar to do it. She might have been angry with me, but I was still her baby sister. Sienna never would have allowed me to be kept by a Vandar Raas, especially one known as the Deranged Warlord. And especially once she'd heard about the curse and the deal I'd made.

It didn't matter, I told myself. He'd still kept secrets from me, and I despised secrets. The one thing I'd actually believed about Vassim was that he would keep his word. But he'd been keeping me in the dark, all while pretending to care about me. Tears pricked the backs of my eyes. All he really cared about was breaking his stupid curse and keeping me with him long enough to do it. How could I believe any of it had been real when I knew what he'd been willing to do to keep me clueless?

"Are you okay?" Baru whispered.

I swiped at my nose, glad that it was pitch dark, and he couldn't see the tears snaking down my cheeks. Before I could answer, the transport jostled roughly. We'd snuck onto one of the ships in the back so we wouldn't be seen, but it was clear the warriors were now boarding it. My heart raced, fearful that we'd be discovered and maybe even more fearful that we wouldn't, and I'd fly right off the warbird and from Raas Vassim's life forever.

Shouts went up outside our closet, the booming voices rattling the metal door. Then the engines rumbled under our feet and the entire vessel vibrated. The Neebix boy muttered some version of a prayer next to me, and Furb had woken, his fur puffing up in my hands.

"No turning back now," I said to myself, feeling the slight drop as the ship lifted off the floor of the hangar bay.

This was only my second trip in a transport ship, and although I'd been living in a huge spaceship, I was reminded that flying was still new to me. And it still made my stomach roil. I pressed my lips together as the sharp tang of bile tickled the back of my throat. The last thing I wanted to do was vomit all over myself in a closet. Even though it was too dark to see anything, I closed my eyes and concentrated on taking deep breaths. I also concentrated on *not* thinking about the fact that I was currently flying through space.

Think about Sienna, I told myself. *Soon you'll be able to see her and apologize and explain everything.*

After everything that had happened, I had to remind myself that my sister was most likely upset about what I'd done back on our home world. Considering the crazy turn my life had taken, I had to remember that me betraying her was probably fresh in her mind.

Was what I'd done to my sister the same as what I was now furious at Vassim for doing? No. I shook my head, then my shoulder sagged. What I'd done had been worse, and it had almost gotten her hurt. The only thing Raas Vassim had hurt was my pride and my trust in him.

Before I could second-guess my plan of a joyful reunion with my angry sister, the ship jolted hard. Baru grabbed my arm, and Furb's tail swung out, the spikes snagging on my dress.

"What was that?" I asked. "Is that how these things land?"

"Not as far as I know," Baru said, his hand trembling.

Another jolt sent us both against the wall hard, and then we were falling toward the ceiling. I lifted my free hand over my head to keep from hitting but then we were falling back down again.

"We're flipping," Baru said. "We must have been hit and lost nav controls."

Now I grabbed his shaking hand. I hadn't even considered the possibility that taking a ship down to the planet during a battle with the empire might result in us dying. I'd never get a chance to see my sister or see Raas Vassim again. As furious as I still was with him, the thought of dying without seeing him made me feel even sicker.

Shouts came from outside the door as the ship continued to jerk, but it finally stopped spinning. Just as I was about to tell Baru that the worst of it was over, the ship slammed to a sudden stop and we were both knocked to the floor.

I stayed down. We were no longer flying, but the transport was rocking strangely. The shouts from outside hadn't lessened, which was both a good and bad sign. It was good because it meant that everyone was still alive. It was bad because their shouts did not sound victorious.

"Maybe we're on the planet," the apprentice suggested.

"But we're rocking."

Suddenly, cool water rushed around my feet, and I leapt up, jerking the boy with me. "We crashed into water. We have to get out of here."

After fumbling with the door for a moment, I pushed it open. Light flooded in and made me shield my eyes. The Vandar ship wasn't bright, but the closet had been pitch-dark, and there was now sunlight streaming in from the ship's cockpit.

"Come on." I pulled Baru as I waded through the ankle-deep water that streamed in the ship. The ramp was open, and the raiders had all left, their heads bobbing in the water as they swam away.

A quick peek from the ship told me that we'd landed in the middle of some sort of lake, the water a vivid shade of sea-green. Wispy trees lined the black banks not too far away.

"We have to swim for it," Baru said, tugging me toward the opening as the water rose to my knees.

"I can't," I said, panic clawing at my throat. "I can't swim."

Baru's eyes widened, then he squared his small shoulders. "Don't worry. I can take you." He spun me around and crossed an arm over my chest, pulling us both into the water on our backs. "Just don't drop that Gerwyn."

I was too terrified to reply as Baru began to slowly kick us away from the ship and toward the shore. Furb was a mass of soaking-wet fur, but he didn't struggle as I held him out of the water. After a while, the water lapped at my chin, and the boy's breathing was heavy and ragged.

"Are you okay?" I asked as more water splashed into my mouth.

"Almost there," he gasped.

I didn't try to crane my neck around to see just how close we were, even though I knew we were sinking. "Let me go, Baru. You're going to drown."

"No one is going to drown today." A heavy arm replaced the boy's spindly one, and my body rose above the water again. Before I could recover from the shock of the deep voice reverberating in my ear, I was being dragged onto the shore.

Raas Vassim knelt beside me. "I would have thought you learned your lesson the first time you stowed away on a ship."

CHAPTER TWENTY-EIGHT

Vassim

Water streamed off Juliette's body as I deposited her on the black sand, her thin dress plastered to her skin. Despite my fury, I couldn't keep my gaze from roaming over her curves on display, or the irritation that the sight was not for my eyes only.

"What are you doing here?" she asked, gaping up at me.

I pulled off my boots and let water pour from them. "I believe I'm the one who should be asking you that question."

Her cheeks flushed, but before she argued with me, a look of panic crossed her face. "Where's Baru?"

I jerked my head toward the Neebix apprentice, who another warrior was helping onto the shore. "He's fine. He was doing an admirable job of swimming you to safety."

Juliette placed the Gerwyn on the ground, and the little creature shook himself hard, his gold fur poofing out around him. "We were sinking before you grabbed me."

"I know." I dragged both hands through my hair and let the water drip down my back. "How do you not swim? Your home world has a large body of water."

She wrinkled her nose. "The shallows are full of sea creatures and kelp. No one swims in there. How do you know how to swim?"

"Our horde once landed on an aquatic planet. It was either swim or sink." I waved a hand at my warriors on the beach and the last few cutting sharp strokes through the water. "All my raiders can swim."

Baru staggered over, sinking down onto the sand beside Juliette.

She put an arm around his shoulders. "Thank you for saving me."

"I didn't save you." He shook his head but didn't look up at me. "The Raas did."

"I only brought her the last bit. You were the one who got her off the sinking transport and almost the entire way," I told him. "I owe you a debt of gratitude."

He finally met my eyes. "I thought you'd be angry at me for not stopping her from getting on the transport."

I shifted my gaze back to Juliette. "That is entirely her fault, and I am only angry at her for behaving so recklessly."

"Recklessly?" Her mouth fell open, but she looked at Baru. "Can you tell the Raas that I only did this because he lied to me?"

Baru's eyes went to me and then back to Juliette.

"I did not lie to you," I said. "I did not tell you information that might upset you."

She shot a menacing look at me but still only spoke to the Neebix boy. "Tell the Raas that of course I'd be upset if I knew that he was in contact with my sister's ship and didn't let me talk to her or join her."

Baru opened his mouth and then lowered his voice. "Do you really wish for me to repeat that?"

"You could not have joined her, and I knew that would have caused you distress."

"Why couldn't I have joined her?" She narrowed her eyes at me for a moment before looking away. "Does the Raas think that it's because of the curse I'm supposed to break?"

My apprentice's face paled and the voices on the beach hushed. The curse—and my accompanying madness—was not something that was discussed by my crew, at least not in front of me.

"You could not have joined her because you made a deal with me, or do you forget your promises so quickly?"

Pink blotches appeared on her cheeks and she leapt up. "I don't forget anything, Raas. I've kept up my end of our deal more than I ever intended to. Were you ever planning to let me go? You said that bedding me wouldn't create the mating marks you so desperately need, but that's not true, is it?"

Now warriors were silently moving away from us, while Baru's nubby horns flamed red.

"It is not *all* that is needed," I said.

"The Raas should tell me the truth," she said to Baru. "He never intended to tell my sister that he had me because he knew she would come for me, and then his plan to bed me long enough to produce mating marks would be ruined." She swiveled her head to me. "Was I ever more than that to you?"

All the fight drained from me as I watched her heaving in ragged breaths. "Juliette—"

"It doesn't matter," she snapped, turning and stomping off, her small feet kicking up dark granules of sand behind her.

The apprentice let out a breath, clearly glad he was no longer in the middle of the argument, but the Gerwyn scampered after Juliette.

I hated that she'd been right about my intentions. I had avoided revealing her presence to the bounty hunters because I did think her sister would insist on her return. Not only did I not want to have conflict with allies like the Dothveks and their crew, but I also hadn't wanted to risk losing Juliette. At first, it had been because of the curse. I'd needed her if I was to have any chance to break it. But then it had become about her. I couldn't stand the thought of losing her.

I'd grown used to her greeting me when I returned to my quarters and sharing my bed. Having someone to fuss over my wounds and surprise me with sweet breads had been much preferable to returning to an empty room that held only memories of restless sleep and promised only tormented nights, or time spent subjecting myself to painful torture to keep me awake. And being inside her had been like nothing I'd ever experienced before, her warm heat like a home I'd never known I'd wanted so desperately.

She was also right that I couldn't give her up now. Even if she never took my marks. Juliette was a part of me, and I needed her by my side. I just had to explain it to her and hope she felt some small measure of what I did.

I tramped off after her, not knowing exactly how to deal with a furious female. I couldn't challenge her to battle, even though in her current state she might very well accept and try to kill me.

Before I'd gotten very far into the sparse woods edging the beach, there was a blast behind me. I looked over my shoulder and saw red laser fire pelting the exposed hull of our sinking transport. The Zagrath knew our ship had fallen and they now knew where we were.

"Off the beach!" I called out, waving for my raiders to follow me into the woods where it would be harder to track us. Within moments, heavy boots were crunching through the underbrush as my warriors ran away from the weapons fire coming from above. Baru was in the thick of the group, being hustled along by two raiders on either side of him.

I resumed tracking Juliette, although now I was running. When I spotted her stomping angrily ahead of me with Furb under her arm, I didn't slow to explain anything. I bent low and scooped her up, throwing her over my shoulder and barely breaking stride as I continued to run away from the blasts, which sounded like they were no longer focused on the sinking ship.

She slapped my bare back with one palm. "Hey! What the hell do you think you're doing?"

"Saving you from being shot by the empire."

"You can't just carry me around like a sack of grain." She hit me again. "I can walk, you know."

"Not fast enough." As I said this, an explosion to one side of us sent half of a tree flying into the air and the other half was scorched black from the laser.

Juliette shrieked, and the Gerwyn's tail flailed, stinging my shoulder with its spikes.

"They're shooting at us?"

"That's what I was trying to tell you," I said, more to myself than to her.

I didn't stop running until the woods had thickened, and the firing had stopped. The air was cooler, and the scent of scorched wood no longer followed us. I couldn't see any other Vandar, and even the pounding of their footsteps was hard to hear. It might take some time to reassemble my raiders, but at least I'd gotten Juliette away from danger.

I swung her down from my shoulder and placed her in front of a wide tree covered in pale, curling bark. "We should be safe—"

She interrupted me with a sharp slap across my face. "That's for keeping secrets from me."

I wasn't as startled by the pain of my stinging cheek as I was the hurt in her eyes. They glittered as she glared at me, and her chin quivered even as she obviously fought to keep from crying.

"I only did it because I couldn't lose you."

"Because of that stupid curse."

"No." I put a hand on her waist and jerked her to me. "Because I cannot bear the thought of being without you."

Her mouth fell open, and a tear slipped from the corner of one eye. Then she snaked a hand around my neck and pulled my mouth to hers.

Despite being shocked again by Juliette, I sank into the kiss, wrapping my arms around her waist and lifting her feet off the ground. When I put her down, a throaty chuckle made me jerk away. It hadn't come from her.

"You remind me very much of another couple I knew," the small creature with nut-brown skin and colorful horns said as he stepped into the clearing.

CHAPTER TWENTY-NINE

Juliette

"Who are you?" As soon as the words spilled from my lips, I regretted their bluntness.

The stocky little alien didn't seem offended, though. He merely smiled and laughed again, a warm rumble that made me want to smile. I didn't know much about different alien species, but I instantly liked this Carlogian with his elaborate outfit of perfectly tailored clothes in sumptuous fabrics. Even though the buttons on his vest sparkled gold, and a velvety, green scarf billowed around his neck, he was not intimidating or arrogant. He actually seemed quite fatherly.

"I am Fenrey."

"You're Carlogian," Raas Vassim said, more a statement than a question.

Fenrey's heavily lined face crinkled as he grinned at us. "Correct, Vandar."

"And you know I'm Vandar."

An eager nod and an even wider smile. "Oh, yes. I'm very familiar with the Vandar." He tilted his head, his colorfully striped horns glinting in the light. "Unless I'm mistaken, you are a Raas."

Vassim inclined his head in a small bow. "I am Raas Vassim, and this is Juliette."

"Yes, yes. We're very familiar with Vandar-human pairings." He chuckled again and waved for us to follow him as he turned. "We expected the Vandar to come, but we didn't expect you."

"We were the closest horde," the Raas said, not making any move to follow. "Where are you taking us, Carlogian?"

"Fenrey," the alien corrected as he stopped and turned. "I'm taking you to our village, but we need to go the long way, since the planet is overrun by imperial soldiers." He wrinkled his already-wrinkled nose. "I apologize in advance for taking you in through the tunnels, but it can't be helped."

"Tunnels? You live underground?"

Fenrey seemed to notice that we hadn't moved and sighed. "Oh, dear. I haven't explained very well, have I?"

"We know that your planet was liberated by the Vandar before and we received your distress call, but when we arrived there was a fleet of Zagrath ships to greet us."

Fenrey's large, brown eyes grew even more round. "You don't think we lured you here under false pretense?" He pressed a hand to his puffy scarf. "Oh, goodness. I can see how it might look like that."

"We believe Zagrath duplicity and cunning much more quickly than we believe your people would collaborate with them," Vassim said.

The Carlogian's expression darkened. "After they enslaved our planet and put our children to work in mines, we would rather die than provide any kind of aid to the empire."

"Then we are in agreement," the Raas said. "But they may have reengaged your planet to draw out the Vandar, especially since they know you were assisted once before by a horde."

"Two hordes." Fenrey held up two stubby fingers. "Raas Kratos and Raas Kaalek. They're brothers, you know. Such nice boys."

Vassim's brows lifted at the description of his fellow Raas'. "Raas Kratos no longer leads a horde. It is now under control of his *majak*, Bron, but Raas Kaalek is still very much in the skies."

"I'm glad to hear it. We owe the Vandar a great debt of gratitude, and I'm afraid it will be greater after this."

The Raas grunted as if dismissing the concept of the debt. "Tell us what transpired."

"Of course." Fenrey fluttered a hand in front of him. "When the other two hordes left us after repelling the empire so forcefully, they left us a communications system so we could send word for help if we ever needed it again. It also transmitted a Vandar signal, which was intended to warn the empire from returning."

"Which did not work," Vassim said.

"It worked for a while. Since the mines were destroyed in the battle, we thought they had no reason to return. They couldn't rebuild them before the Vandar would arrive and we believed that was enough of a deterrent." Fenrey tapped his foot on the ground, the underbrush crackling. "And it is true they haven't touched the mines since their ship entered orbit."

"What have they done?" I asked.

The little horned alien looked up at me and shrugged. "Nothing really, aside from make their presence known. Like I said, their ship entered our orbit and then they sent smaller vessels to the surface, but as of yet they haven't done any of the things they did during the last invasion. They haven't rounded up the younger males, or retaken the garrison in the village."

"Which gives weight to the theory that all of this is being done to lure the Vandar into an ambush." Raas Vassim tipped his head up to peer at the sky.

Fenrey pressed his hands to his cheeks. "I would never forgive myself if we were the reason that the Vandar were destroyed by the empire."

Now Raas Vassim laughed, but it was not warm and mirthful. "The Vandar cannot be defeated so easily, but maybe we can turn this strategy around on our enemy."

"I like the sound of that," Fenrey said.

"The empire has no idea that we have figured out their strategy. They also do not know how many hordes we have and how many allies. Not only do the Vandar fight for you, but we also brought the Valox resistance, and a bounty hunter crew."

Fenrey's face lit up with delight. "The bounty hunters are back? Oh, I do like them."

Mention of the bounty hunter crew made me think about my sister. "You haven't seen them on the surface yet?"

Fenrey shook his head. "No, but they're very good at stealth, those Dothveks. They come from a sand planet, you know. And the women who fly with them are quite impressive on their own. I wouldn't be surprised if they're here, and we just haven't detected them yet."

Even though my sister was now a part of their crew, I knew almost nothing about the bounty hunters, which made me flush with embarrassment. I'd avoided the battle they'd joined in on when my home world had been attacked, and my attempt to stowaway on their ship had not exactly worked out.

The Raas put an arm around me. "We should probably get out of sight. Unfortunately, our arrival on the planet was not so stealthy."

"We saw your ship fall from the sky," the Carlogian said, as he led us through the forest. "And the imperial ships fire on it once it was done. We didn't know if there would be survivors, which was why I alerted Coxley."

"What's a Coxley?" I asked.

The alien chuckled. "Not a *what*, a *he*. Coxley is our healer." He swiveled his head when they reached an opening in the woods where the greenery and crawling vines were tamped down. "And I left him right here when we heard you two arguing."

My flush deepened at the reminder that I'd yelled at Vassim before I'd slapped him hard across the cheek.

"I'm here, Fenrey." The voice was slightly higher pitched, but when the other Carlogian appeared through a thicket, I was pleasantly surprised to see Baru by his side. "I was helping this young fellow. He seemed to have gotten separated from his friends..." His words died off when he saw the Raas, and he emitted a squeak before clamping his mouth shut.

"This is Raas Vassim, Coxley." Fenrey nudged the Carlogian with dark curly hair between his colorfully striped horns. "He and his horde have arrived to help us."

Coxley's large eyes, which were a startling shade of blue, blinked a few times as he nodded, finally clearing his throat. "Good to meet you."

"I'm Juliette," I said, leaving the Raas' side to walk over to the Neebix boy and give him a once-over. "Are you okay?"

"He had a cut on his leg, which I took care of," the healer said, smoothing his hands down the front of his long dark jacket and smiling at me.

"It was like magic," Baru whispered, pulling up the hem of his pants to reveal a faint pink gash that had knitted together. "Even faster than the waters the Vandar use."

Coxley's coppery-brown cheeks took on a faint hint of pink. "The plants on our planet are quite medicinal."

"We should get these three back to the village," Fenrey said. "There are too many imperial soldiers in these woods. Besides," he cut his eyes to the dress that still clung wet to my skin. "I need to get this poor girl into some proper clothes."

"Fenrey is a tailor." Coxley kept his eyes up, purposefully not looking at the fabric plastered to my skin that was no doubt revealing.

"Oh." I tugged the sagging neckline of my wet dress. "It would be nice to get out of this."

"Don't you worry," Fenrey said over his shoulder. "I'll whip you up something much more flattering, dear."

Coxley glanced over his shoulder and tugged a leather case closer to his chest. "If you ask me, one imperial soldier is too many."

Raas Vassim thumped him on the back, almost sending the little alien flying. "You and I are of one mind, healer."

Coxley let out another strangled squeak and looked up at the Raas with a shaky smile. "Oh, good."

The Raas put a hand to the small of my back as the two Carlogians led us through the dense woods, the spindly trees rising high with branches at the top that created a leafy canopy. For a while, there was nothing but the sounds of our feet crunching leaves, and the occasional bird call, as Baru trudged along beside me, and Furb slept in my arms.

Then Vassim tensed, his hand moving from my back to the hilt of his axe. "We're being followed."

CHAPTER THIRTY

Vassim

The two Carlogians froze in mid-step, Fenrey twisting his head around to look at me. "You are sure?"

I gave a scant nod. "Behind us. Not many, but they're moving quickly."

"We should run for it," the nervous healer said, shifting his case around to his hip.

"They'll catch us," I said. "Or shoot at us."

"Then what do we do?" Although Juliette's voice trembled, she squared her shoulders as if bracing herself for what was coming.

I held Fenrey's gaze for a moment. "I need you to get Juliette and Baru to safety. I'll join you later." I doubted I'd be able to join them at all, but I didn't want to frighten Juliette.

He pressed his lips together and bobbed his head up and down sharply, understanding my meaning.

"No way," Juliette said, shifting Furb to one hip. "I know what you're doing. You're sacrificing yourself to save the rest of us."

I took her by the shoulders, giving her a little shake. "Do you want all of us to be killed or taken prisoner, because that's what will happen if you all don't go now."

She inhaled sharply, her brow furrowed, but she shook her head.

"Do not have such little faith in me," I said, managing a small smile. "I am a Vandar Raas, after all. I have met with worse and survived." I wanted to crush my lips to hers and tell her all the things I'd meant to, but there was no time. "I *will* see you again."

She opened her mouth, but no words came out, only a strangled sob.

I released her and stepped back, drawing my battle axe. "Please, Juliette. Go!"

With a final tortured, backward glance, she allowed Baru and Coxley to pull her away from me, and the group stumbled off through the woods.

I turned away from the sound of their retreat, holding my axe at the ready, my ears attuned to the noise of imperial soldiers advancing. My raiders were spread throughout the forest, but calling them would only alert the Zagrath to my location. And if I ran in a different direction, they might not follow me and instead catch up to Juliette. I gritted my teeth. I could not let that happen. Whatever happened to me, I needed for her to be safe.

Quickly scanning the trees and undergrowth, I noted that the trees were not as willowy as the ones near the beach, although they were still not wide enough for me to hide behind, and their branches were too high up to climb. There would be no ambush from above for me, and no leaping from a hiding spot. A head-on battle, then.

I shifted my axe from one hand to the next, impatient to fight. It had been a long time since I'd fought solo. Vandar always raided as a finely-tuned horde, warriors in lock step with shields linked. We trained together, fought together, died together, and lived for eternity together in Zedna with the warrior gods of old. I did not fear death, but I did not want to die without my Vandar warriors by my side.

When the black-helmeted soldiers appeared, their smoke-blue uniforms unmarked by signs of battle, I almost smiled. There were only three of them, and although they pointed blasters at my chest, I'd seen worse odds.

"Drop your weapon, Vandar." The voice was muffled from behind the shiny, black helmet.

I clenched the handle tighter, careful not to telegraph my movement, but also subtly angling my foot so I could lunge easily. "No."

"We don't want to kill you," another soldier said.

"Then that's where we differ." I bared my teeth at them, my heart pounding. "I very much want to kill you for all the pain you've wrought across the galaxy."

The soldiers glanced at each other, and I used their momentary distraction to my advantage, lunging forward and swinging my axe up. The blade sliced through one of the soldier's arms, sending it spiraling into the air and blood spurting out from the stump above the elbow.

With a bellow of pain, the wounded soldier collapsed to his knees, clutching at his severed arm. The other two backed up like Rengli beetles scuttling away from light. I didn't wait for them to respond by firing, instead spinning around and taking off the kneeling soldier's head with another lightning-fast slash of my axe.

One down, I thought. Two to go.

A flash of movement drew my eye and made me pivot toward it. That was when electricity jolted through me, making my body contract and spasm. Pain surged through me as I dropped to the ground, unable to lift my axe to defend myself as the two soldiers closed in on me. I finally closed my eyes, the pain making light shoot across the inside of my eyelids and stealing even that bit of relief.

I braced myself for the inevitable blaster shots that would end my life and send me to the glorious afterlife of a Vandar warrior, my mind already envisioning the gates of Zedna. But the shots never came. Instead, my arms were jerked behind my back and bound, the bindings tight around my wrists. Another rough restraint was wrapped around my shoulders and chest, and I was pulled up to standing.

"I told you we didn't want to kill you," one of the soldiers growled in my ear through the ringing.

"The general wants a Vandar prisoner," another said with a dark laugh as he snatched my axe from me. "Someone to make an example of."

I didn't speak as they pushed me through the woods, using the restraints to tug me forward when I slowed. My legs still shook from the pain of whatever they'd jolted into me, but I managed to stagger forward. My only consolation from the humiliation of being captured by the Zagrath was that Juliette had gotten away. My distraction had worked.

After a while, we reached the black sand beach that I'd started from. But now, instead of being filled with Vandar warriors, Zagrath soldiers swarmed the area, one of their gray transports sitting on the sand at the far end. An imperial officer who wasn't wearing a helmet stalked up as soon as we emerged from the woods. His light brown hair was slicked across a pronounced forehead where sweat beaded.

"You got one!" He eyed me like I was a dangerous creature, which I was. "What's your name, Vandar."

"Vassim," I said, spitting at his feet.

"Barbarians," he muttered, making a face and taking a step back. "I am General Jamose of the Zagrath Empire. You are trespassing on Zagrath territory, which is a capital crime."

I grinned coldly at him. "Are you going to kill me, Jamose?"

He twitched his shoulders. "Generals do not execute prisoners of war, although I should kill you right here as punishment for all the destruction you brutes have caused to the empire." His face reddened as he paced in front of me. "You and your cowardly hordes have killed countless Zagrath citizens with your violent attacks on our ships."

"Soldiers," I corrected. "We've killed soldiers, not civilians. You are the ones who enslave innocent alien populations."

"Enslave?" He spluttered the words out, spittle flying from his mouth. "We colonize planets and allow primitive societies to become a part the glorious empire."

"Against their will."

"If they are too simple-minded to know what is best for them, that is not the fault of the empire." He waved a hand at me. "Why am I debating with a half-naked brute?" He narrowed his eyes at me. "You will be taken to the imperial headquarters, Vandar, where you will be tried publicly and then executed for your crimes."

"So a fair Zagrath trial?"

He clenched his jaw and fisted his hands, as if he wished to hit me but was too afraid to try. "All Vandar are guilty." He threw his shoulders back, puffing out his slender chest. "I look forward to watching your execution."

"If you live that long," I said just loud enough for him to hear the dark rumble of my words.

He jerked back as if he'd been slapped, then turned and stomped away. "Put him in the energy pincers until we can leave the planet."

At least I wasn't being taken off the planet right away, I thought as I was dragged over to a round, steel platform, with two curved arms arching up on either side from the base. There was still time to escape or fight my way out.

When they put me onto the platform and flipped a switch at the bottom, all thoughts of escape left my mind as energy surged through me once again.

CHAPTER THIRTY-ONE

Juliette

"We have to go back for him," I said, after I'd been rushed down an underground tunnel and climbed up a ladder to a cozy dwelling that belonged to Fenrey.

Fenrey bustled me into a room with a large table covered in papers that curled up around the corners, with bits of fabric straight-pinned onto them. Candles burned in sconces on the wall, filling the room with the scent of tallow and smoke, and sending a warm glow flickering across the dark-brown walls. He led me to an upholstered chair and patted it. "First, you have to get out of those wet clothes before you catch your death."

"Wet clothes won't cause your death," Coxley muttered, earning him a sharp look from the other Carlogian.

"We can't have her running all over the place in that soggy scrap of a dress." Fenrey hurried behind the large table, tugging swaths of fabric down from where they hung in bolts on the wall. "No one ever mounted a rescue in an outfit like that."

I tried not to feel too self-conscious as he fluttered a wrinkled hand at me. The dress hadn't been too bad before I'd taken a swim in the lake, but it did look like a saggy mess now. I crossed my arms over my chest, hoping to cover some of my bare flesh that was exposed by the drooping neckline.

"Don't mind him," Coxley whispered. "He's just tense because of the Zagrath."

Fenrey slammed down a pair of shiny, gold scissors. "Of course I'm tense. Last time, they took my son to the mines, and now the Vandar are here again, but we have a missing Raas."

"I won't be going back to the mines," a younger Carlogian said, as he descended the staircase that ran up one wall to a second level.

"Lebben." Fenrey jumped when he saw the man who looked like a less-wizened version of himself. "You shouldn't be down here?"

"Why not?" The Carlogian put his hands on his hips and stared down at his father. "I hope you don't think I'm going to sit this out."

Fenrey closed his eyes for a moment and his small shoulders sagged. "I couldn't live with myself if you…"

"Nothing will happen to me, Da." Lebben walked around the table and put a hand on his father's brown, nubby jacket. "But you're crazy if you think I'm going to let you be the only one in this family to take risks."

"We started the resistance to keep our families safer," Fenrey said, but there was little fight left in his voice.

"And we will be safe once we kick out the empire again."

"Hear, hear!" Coxley clapped his hands and ignored Fenrey's glare.

The tailor finally sighed and turned back to his table. "Fine, but we can't do anything until I get this child in some more appropriate clothes. It's beyond me what these Vandar put on their females."

Lebben turned to me. "You're Vandar?"

Baru choked back a laugh. "She's human. See?" He waved a hand toward my backside. "No tail."

"Right." Lebben's face flushed slightly but he still looked at me with fascination. "But you are with the Vandar?"

"Sort of," I said. How did I explain how and why I'd come to be on the Vandar horde ship without shocking everyone? I definitely wasn't going to tell them about the curse and the witch, and the deal I'd made with Raas Vassim.

"She stowed away on board Raas Vassim's warbird," Baru said, preempting any explanation I might have thought up. "So he decided to keep her instead of putting her out an airlock, which is what he'd usually do with stowaways."

A hush descended over the room. Okay, maybe I could have explained it better. "The Raas was never going to put me out an airlock. He's actually returning me to my home planet soon."

Fenrey's bushy eyebrows shot up and almost disappeared under his mass of brown, curly hair. He'd seen me kissing Vassim, so I doubted he believed that. Even I thought the words sounded like a lie on my tongue.

"You aren't his mate?" he asked.

I shook my head, while Baru nodded. "She might as well be. The Raas spends all his free time with her, instead of wandering the halls. He even got her a pet."

As if he knew he was being discussed, Furb wiggled on my lap, stretching his short legs out in front of him and opening one eye.

"But you wish to risk yourself to go find this Vandar who is not your mate?" Coxley asked.

"He would do the same for me," I said, knowing for certain that was true.

"She's right," Fenrey said, cutting the fabric he'd stretched across the table. "He sacrificed himself so we could get away. We can't let him be killed by the Zagrath."

"If they caught him, he might already—" Coxley said.

Fenrey cut him off. "No sense in guessing about what may or may not have happened. We need to regroup, get the resistance together, and find the Vandar."

"No need." Another Carlogian pushed through the heavy drape separating the room from the back of the house and the tunnel entrance. "I know what happened to the Vandar."

"Taiko." Lebben greeted the Carlogian, who had a wiry tuft of russet-colored hair that stood up between the striped horns that curled around his ears. "How do you know about the Vandar?"

The skinny little alien scratched nervously at his arms as he surveyed the room. "I was in the wood looking for good trees."

"Taiko is the village's carpenter," Coxley whispered to me out of the corner of his mouth.

"You know you shouldn't have been out there alone," Fenrey scolded. "Not with the empire roaming these parts."

Taiko scratched more vigorously. "I know, but I need some more planks to shore up the tunnels, especially if we'll be needing them again. Anyway, I saw a Vandar fighting against some imperial soldiers."

My heart stuttered. "Was he wearing black armor on one shoulder and a strap that crossed his chest?"

The carpenter nodded. "He took off one soldier's arm then his head before they brought him down."

Cold fear slid across my skin as Baru sank down onto the arm of my chair. "What do you mean 'brought him down?'"

"They didn't kill him. They shot this little red dart into him, and he started twitching something awful. It was like he was being electrocuted the way he fell on the ground and convulsed."

A wave of nausea swept over me, but I pressed my lips together and sucked in a deep breath, even though the warmth of the room and the scent of the candles didn't help. At least he wasn't dead. That was the important thing.

"Then what?" Lebben asked.

"They tied him up and marched him away, toward the ebony sand beach." Taiko stopped scratching his arms and dropped them by his side. "I came back here so we could come up with a plan to free him."

"Good thinking." Fenrey whipped a needle out of a pin cushion and began sticking the fabric on the table. "The faster we can get him back, the better."

"If there's a plan to be made, I hope you'll let us help." A woman with a head full of wild, red curls stepped from behind the curtain, causing Taiko to jump. "And I hope it's okay we used the tunnel."

"Tara!" Fenrey's face brightened, and he dropped both his needle and fabric onto the table, rushing over to pull her into a hug.

A hulking Vandar warrior draped with black leather straps and armor on both of his shoulders joined her. "I hope you know that you're the only male I would allow to embrace my mate like that."

Tara slapped the Vandar's chest. "Don't be such an ass, Kaalek."

Coxley made a small squeaking noise and took a step back.

"As you see, she still doesn't obey me," Kaalek said with a grin.

"Raas Kaalek," Fenrey released the female and threw his arms around the Vandar Raas. "It is good to see you."

The Raas patted the Carlogian on the back. "You didn't think we'd miss the chance to kill Zagrath, did you? My horde is at your disposal, as is my axe."

"What we need to do is save Raas Vassim," I said, my voice rising over the warm greetings.

Raas Kaalek swiveled his gaze to me. "Raas *Lunori* is here?"

CHAPTER THIRTY-TWO

Juliette

"He's not deranged," I said, bristling at the offhanded way Raas Kaalek had referred to Vassim. "He's cursed."

The Raas strode over to where I sat, peering down at me and making me wonder if the Raas' went to a special training on how to be intimidating. "You know Raas Vassim?"

"Know him?" Baru laughed. "She's his—"

"I'm a guest on his warbird," I said, shooting the Neebix boy a death glare, which resulted in his horns flushing. "And I promise you he's not crazy or mad, or any of that."

Raas Kaalek looked me up and down. "How did another human female find her way onto one of our warbirds?"

"Stop bothering the poor thing," Tara said, pushing him aside. "You're being a bully, Kaalek."

He growled low. "I am a Vandar. Not a bully."

She rolled her eyes and smiled at me. "Ignore him...?" She paused and let her words trail off in a question.

"I'm Juliette. I'm from Kimithion III."

Raas Kaalek wrinkled his brow. "That planet is notorious for keeping to itself. I've never heard of one of you leaving."

"I'm not the only one," I said before I could stop myself. "My older sister, Sienna, left with one of your kind first."

This made the Raas gape at me, his incredulous expression making it clear he didn't believe me. "A Vandar took a human from your planet? I find that hard to..." He stopped when Tara whirled around and leveled him with a warning gaze.

"Corvak was exiled to my planet," I explained. "He'd been a battle chief on one of your hordes."

Kaalek nodded slowly. "On my elder brother's horde, at least before he hung up his battle axe. Corvak is our cousin through our mother's side. I didn't know him well, but he was said to be a valiant warrior."

"He was, he is," I said. "He readied our planet for an attack by the empire and fought them off with some help."

The Raas scraped a hand through his dark hair. "Exiled? What must he have done for such a fate?" His words seemed meant for himself only, until he looked up at me. "And your sister left with him?"

"Sienna loves fighting almost as much as Corvak. They were perfect together, even if I didn't want to admit it." I swallowed the lump of regret that had formed in my throat. "I heard she took his mating marks before they left with a group of bounty hunters to continue fighting the empire."

Tara studied me, her smile kind. "You and your sister fought before she left?"

I nodded, too afraid to speak with a sob threatening to escape.

"I get it. I have a younger sister. We got under each other's skin all the time, but that didn't mean we still weren't sisters."

"I tried to follow her and explain everything, but I snuck onto the wrong ship."

"You stowed away on Raas Vassim's ship?" Kaalek voice held a hint of amusement. "Well, that explains why you're here with him." His eyes drifted to my neck and exposed chest. "Although you aren't…?"

"No, we aren't," I said, maybe a bit too quickly.

Tara raised an eyebrow, but didn't comment.

"I don't think it matters why I'm here, or how I got to be on Raas Vassim's ship. What matters is that he stayed behind to fight off the imperial soldiers so we could escape, and now he's been taken by them. We have to get him back."

"Being with a Vandar horde has rubbed off on you, human," Raas Kaalek said. "But I agree with you. We cannot let a Raas of the Vandar be held by the empire. Not when he is such a valuable prize for them."

"What do you mean?" I asked.

"The empire have never captured a Vandar raider, and certainly not one of our Raas'. Knowing their love for a display of might, I suspect they will not kill him here. They will take him somewhere and make a spectacle of his death."

I sank back onto the chair, the thought of Vassim being killed taking all the wind out of me.

"But that's not going to happen," Tara said. "They can't take him anywhere, with two hordes battling it out with the empire overhead. It's too dangerous to get a transport through that. Kaalek and I took a huge risk flying down, and we took the smallest ship possible. No way our horde ships would let an imperial transport through."

"Which means we have time to rescue him." Fenrey unfurled the garment he'd been stitching as they talked. It was a moss-green jumpsuit with a draping, cowl neckline, and even from across the room, I could tell that it had been tailored to fit my curves. "Which means we need a plan, and we need it fast."

Coxley tapped a finger to his chin. "No time for explosives this go-around."

"No need." Raas Kaalek took a step closer to the healer and threw an arm around his shoulders. Coxley looked pained as the huge Vandar thumped his arm. "This mission needs to be about stealth not a loud distraction, and I think the doctor here can help us with that."

"Me?" Coxley asked, his voice high. "What can I do?"

"You administer sedatives, correct?"

Coxley peered up at the Raas, his bright-blue eyes widening with understanding. "If the situation calls for it."

"Trust us." Tara winked at him. "The situation calls for it."

Coxley's cheeks once again tinged with pink. "You wish to sedate the imperial soldiers? In the past, our village chemist has ground a powder into their drinks."

Kaalek shook his head. "We don't have time for that. We need something faster. Something that can be administered by a needle or dart."

"A dart?" Lebben grinned. "I've got darts from when I was a boy. My friends and I used to play all the time on the side of this building." He stole a glance at Fenrey. "It used to drive my father mad."

Fenrey made a harrumphing sound. "All those tiny holes in the side of my shop."

His son's smile grew as he hurried to the stairs. "I have them upstairs in a box."

Coxley drummed his fingers on the leather case he wore across one shoulder. "I suppose I could fashion something that might work. The sedative itself would have to be highly concentrated."

"We only need to knock them out long enough to get the Raas away," Kaalek said, releasing his grip on the healer and putting a hand on the hilt of his axe. "If they wake, I will take them out."

"It sounds like we have the start of a plan." Fenrey stepped out from behind his table with the garment and pointed at me. "While they work on darts and strategy, it's time for you to look a little bit less like a damsel in distress."

I eyed Tara, who looked every bit the warrior, in her snug pants and leather vest with a blaster on her hip and a blade strapped to her thigh. I'd never look as tough as her, but Coxley was right. I couldn't help save Vassim in a dress that had belonged to a pleasurer. It was time to stop looking like a timid female from Kimithion III and start looking like a woman who could hold her own with a Vandar warlord.

Hold on, Vassim, I thought as I followed the little Carlogian to the back of his shop and the others hunched over the large worktable discussing the best route to the beach. *We're coming.*

CHAPTER THIRTY-THREE

Vassim

The energy field that held me upright between the two metal arches didn't hurt like the shock that had knocked me out in the forest. It did, however, make it impossible for me to move. Even curling my fingers into a fist was impossible, and after a while I gave up and let my body go limp.

The indignity of being held captive by the Zagrath burned like raw fury inside me, as I watched the helmeted guards pace around me. Occasionally, they would laugh and jeer at me but mostly they talked with each other, making plans to drink after the battle or hoping to meet up with some female at a Zagrath outpost or colony.

At least my rage kept me awake. Now was not the time for me to slip into one of my torturous nightmares that left me drained and exhausted. Despite the pain from their energy weapons, sleep still threatened to overtake me if I didn't keep my anger stoked hot, the desire to kill the Zagrath prickling like fire across my skin. I could not slip into madness, not if I was to escape and return to Juliette, so I focused what was left of my strength on the enemy and their movements.

It was their general I watched most closely. He was impatient to leave the planet, unbuttoning his uniform jacket and swiping at sweat on his large forehead caused by the humidity. But every time he received a communication from the imperial battleships above telling him to stay put, he would stomp around and kick at the sand. He reminded me more of a child than a military leader, and not for the first time I wondered how the Zagrath had gained so much power when their people were so weak and cowardly.

When darkness started to fall, he let out a torrent of Zagrath curses, stalking over to where I was being held and addressing the soldiers guarding me. "We'll have to stay here until morning. Take shifts watching him." His thin upper lip curled. "Not that the brute can move. Still, I do not want him escaping. Not when I'm about to provide a live Vandar to put on trial."

I couldn't move, but I managed to growl, the noise rising above the hum of the energy field. He twitched at the sound, but then laughed. "A barbarian to the end. You Vandar don't disappoint."

I distracted myself by imagining how I was going to kill the general and the soldiers guarding me, deciding that beheading was too quick and merciless. They deserved to lose at least one limb first, perhaps two. The general I might hobble before burying my axe in his chest.

My only comfort aside from imagining their deaths was the knowledge that Juliette had gotten away, along with Baru and the Carlogians. My heart swelled with the knowledge that she was safe and would be taken care of no matter what happened to me.

The imperial soldiers hadn't returned from their scouting missions with Juliette, the Carlogians, or any of my raiders. Not all of the imperial soldiers had returned, though, and I suspected my warriors had taken them out.

If the general suspected the same, he refused to acknowledge it. Instead, he waved his arms and threatened punishment to all those who were late returning. When night fell, his threats became fewer and farther between as half of his contingent of soldiers remained missing. It was a small comfort as I stood immobilized with guards walking around me.

Even as the planet fell into quiet, the only sounds that of bugs chirping into the night and the water lapping the sand, muffled booms continued overhead as the battle in space raged on. I couldn't tip my head back, but I could lift my eyes enough to see the occasional faint red glow high above us, and I knew my *majak* fought on.

After a while, two of my guards sat down with their backs to each other. My legs ached from being forced to stand for so long, but I closed my eyes and thought of Juliette to distract me and keep me from drifting into tumultuous sleep and gut-wrenching nightmares. Her gold hair spilling around her head, her blue eyes wide with wonder and desire, her luscious curves that begged to be caressed. My arousal—and the throb of my cock—might be sweet agony, but it was better than the madness of my dreams. I was so lost in my visions of her that I almost didn't hear the snap of the twig.

My eyes flew open. The guards both on the ground and slowly walking around me hadn't heard it. Their plodding pace hadn't altered, and the seated ones appeared to be close to nodding off.

I swiveled my eyes, trying to see through the darkness into the nearby woods. Had I imagined the sound? It could have been anything—an animal, an imperial soldier finally returning, a Zagrath coming back from relieving himself. But I sensed that it wasn't. It was too quiet to be either a creature or a Zagrath. I suspected it was even too subtle to be one of my bulky raiders, who were not accustomed to moving silently through undergrowth.

When the pacing Zagrath turned away from the forest, flashes of movement jerked them back and two sharp snaps were the only indication of their swift deaths. Even that sound didn't alert the soldiers who'd dozed off on the ground and in a blur of gold, their throats were cut, and they slumped silently to the sand, blood pooling around their heads.

I wasn't completely surprised when Corvak appeared in front of me, his finger to his lips as he knelt at the base of the contraption and disengaged the energy field. My knees gave way once I was no longer being held up by the currents, and Corvak caught me under the arm before I toppled. The two Dothveks who'd dispatched the sleeping guards joined us, nodding to me and glancing over at the imperial transport ship and the rest of the dozing soldiers sprawled on the beach.

"Do you wish us to kill them all, Raas?" Corvak whispered, as he helped me down.

I looked at the bleeding bodies on the sand. As much as I wished to storm the imperial ship and kill the general who'd tormented me, I had more important matters on my mind. I straightened, my strength already returning to me, along with my anger. I tamped it down even as my fingers tingled to swing my axe. "Leave them. They mean nothing."

I followed the Dothveks and Corvak into the forest, walking for a way until we reached a slight opening where the rest of the Dothveks and some of the female bounty hunters were waiting.

"We found your axe, Raas." Corvak handed it to me.

I gratefully took it and hooked it on my belt. "How did you find *me*?"

"These guys are kick-ass trackers," a female with a mane of dark curls said, flashing me a grin. "We saw your ship go down and then we saw the Zagrath ship that followed. By the time we made it to the water, you were being held in that machine."

"Tori is right. We were too late to prevent your capture, so we have been watching at a distance," K'alvek said. "We waited for nightfall to strike."

"Some of your raiders are already at our ship," another gold-skinned Dothvek said, this one with black bands ringing his biceps.

"You ready to join them?" Corvak asked.

"I am grateful to you all," I said, "but before I go to your ship, I need to locate Juliette and the Carlogians."

Corvak looked at me like he hadn't heard right. "Juliette is here?"

"Yes. She followed me to the planet's surface, and as far as I am aware, she is with the Carlogians now."

The Vandar rubbed the side of his head, his expression dark. "You did not take her as a spoil of war, did you, Raas?"

Fury flared inside me at the suggestion, but I shook off the emotion. "I did not take her at all. It is a long story, but she is here with me, and she escaped with some Carlogians. I need to find them and make sure she is safe."

A female stepped forward, her hair pulled up high on her head and her hands on her hips. I recognized her immediately as Corvak's mate and Juliette's sister, Sienna. Her eyes blazed with anger. "What do you mean, my sister is here?"

CHAPTER THIRTY-FOUR

Juliette

My pulse fluttered nervously as I followed behind Raas Kaalek and Tara. It had taken half the night to prepare the sedative darts and plot the best route to the beach, so it was hard for me to be patient and not run headlong through the woods to find Vassim. But I steadied my breath, reminding myself that our best weapon was the element of surprise and tearing through the forest would not help save the Raas.

"Are you okay?" Lebben asked, walking up beside me.

Although his father had protested loudly, he'd insisted on joining the mission, arguing that his years of pelting the side of his father's shop with darts had made him the most skilled in the group. So he walked along with me while the other Carlogians, along with Baru and Furb, stayed behind to ensure that their village wasn't overrun by imperial forces while we were away. At first, Raas Kaalek hadn't wanted me to come, insisting that a rescue mission was no place for an inexperienced human, but once Tara had noticed my resolve, she'd sweet-talked him into it. Still, my stomach roiled as I thought about what we were doing, and how ill-prepared I was for it.

"I'm fine," I said, giving the younger Carlogian a weak smile. "Nervous, but glad to be dressed sensibly for once."

Lebben glanced at the form-fitting jumpsuit that blended in with the trees around me. I didn't know how his father had done it, but he'd sized me up with a glance. The outfit fit me like a glove, and might have been the most comfortable thing I'd ever worn.

"That does work well for blending into the woods. I doubt anyone would see you coming." He looked up. "Aside from your hair."

I'd almost forgotten that my blonde curls were hanging loosely around my shoulders, and I touched a hand to them.

"I actually think my father took that into consideration," Lebben said, reaching around and pulling the draping cowl neck up so that it transformed into a hood that covered my hair.

"Wow." I tugged the fabric so that it brushed the top of my forehead. "You father is really good."

Lebben beamed. "He is. He always wanted me to join him in being a tailor, but I don't have the same passion for it, or his talent."

My heart contracted with an ache for a father as loving as Fenrey, but I managed to smile at Lebben. "What is your passion?"

"Music." Even through the dim moonlight filtering down through the web of leaves above, I could see the pride in the

Carlogian's face. "Mostly Carlogian lute and lyre, but I also compose."

I'd never had a chance to try an instrument, not that music had been a central part of life on my home world. The native Kimitherians couldn't play any instrument easily with their webbed hands, and the warbling sounds they made when they sang had been enough to turn me off music.

"What about you? What do you love to do?" Lebben asked.

Before I could tell him about my baking, Kaalek and Tara stopped short in front of us, and Tara threw back an outstretched arm.

"We're getting close." She hunched over and moved gingerly forward behind Raas Kaalek, who held his battle axe at the ready.

Lebben and I followed them, trying to step where they'd stepped to limit the crunch of vegetation beneath our feet. As we moved forward and the trees became sparser, Lebben shifted his leather satchel, pulling out a handful of darts.

I glanced over at him, noting the tight set of his jaw. He was just as scared as I was, and somehow, that made me feel better.

The moonlight grew brighter as the forest became less dense, and finally I saw glimpses of black sand, and beyond that, the reflective surface of the water. We paused at the edge of the woods. There was little sound, and I was unable to see around Kaalek to look for Vassim. Where would they keep a prisoner before taking him to a larger ship in orbit?

"Someone has beaten us to it," Kaalek said, his voice a low rumble.

My stomach lurched. "What do you mean? Is Raas Vassim…?"

Kaalek stepped out onto the sand and we all followed, peering down at the imperial bodies strewn across the sand. Two lay on the edge of the sand almost as if they were sleeping, but for the awkward angle of their necks. Another two sagged on the ground, dark puddles of blood cradling their heads.

My eyes went to the strange metal apparatus to one side, which Kaalek was now circling as if he were stalking prey. He bent low and examined the base. "This is where they kept the Raas."

I glanced back at the bodies. "Do you think he did all this?"

Kaalek tilted his head. "He is a Raas of the Vandar, but if this machine works the way I suspect it does, I doubt he could have escaped alone."

"We arrived on the planet with other raiders," I said. "They all ran off into the woods when we did. Maybe they came back and rescued him."

"That is likely." Raas Kaalek raised his head to the imperial ship farther down the beach and the soldiers lying on mats beside it. "What is unlikely is that they left imperial survivors."

Tara put a hand on his arm as he made a move to go toward the sleeping Zagrath. "Leave them. We still need to find Raas Vassim and the rest of his raiders."

Kaalek emitted a low growl, casting a malicious glance at the enemy. "The only good Zagrath is a dead one."

Tara patted his arm. "I promise there will be plenty of Zagrath to kill after we've completed our mission, Muscles."

He cut his eyes to her. "You are still an infuriating female."

"Which is why you love me so much."

He swatted her ass with another growl. "It isn't the main reason."

Lebben exchanged a glance with me, and I wondered if Tara and Kaalek remembered we were with them. Before I could clear my throat or back away and give them privacy, a yell shattered the air.

"The prisoner!"

Imperial soldiers were scrambling to their feet and running our way, clearly thinking we were in the middle of freeing Raas Vassim, when in fact, he was long gone. Blaster fire erupted around us, kicking up sand and illuminating us in red light. Raas Kaalek swung his axe up, blocking some of the laser fire with the wide circular blade.

"Get behind me," he called out, pushing Tara back as he ran forward.

Tara screamed his name and a few choice words, but he was already cutting down imperial soldiers as they rushed toward him. I'd never seen a Vandar warrior in action, and I couldn't help gaping as how skillfully he moved. Lebben sprung into action, as well, firing off darts that felled several warriors as they ran. One after another, the Zagrath fell.

More imperial soldiers pounded toward us, and Tara stepped from behind her mate to fire a blaster, despite his bellows for her to stay back. Lebben's aim with his darts was impressive, as was the Vandar's ability to block blaster fire with the blade of his axe. Soon, only a handful of struggling soldiers remained to fight against us. Tara ignored Kaalek's warnings, leaping between him and Lebben to emit a spray of blaster fire that leveled the Zagrath.

I took a step back toward the woods as Kaalek clapped Lebben on the arm and gave his mate a withering look filled with both pride and irritation. That was when an arm snaked around my neck and jerked me off my feet.

"Drop your weapons," the voice said in my ear. "Unless you want her to die."

Kaalek and Tara stared at me—or rather, behind me—as the man who held me breathed heavily, his foul breath hot on my neck.

Tara held up her hands in a show of surrender. "Okay, okay. You must be Captain…?"

"General Jamose," the voice snapped. "I was upset that you took my prisoner, but it looks like you brought me another one. I really don't care which one of you brutes I take back to headquarters for trial and execution."

Kaalek flinched, his face a mask of rage.

"Now lower that axe, and I'll consider letting this woman live."

I spotted a couple of imperial soldiers coming up behind the Raas, my gaze flicking to them. I suspected that as soon as he lowered his axe, we'd all become prisoners of the empire. And Raas Kaalek would be tried and executed, if the general was telling the truth.

"Do it!" Jamose screamed, jabbing the point of the blaster roughly into my temple.

Raas Kaalek glanced at Tara, who nodded, and he began to slowly lower his axe. Tara also gave a subtle nod to Lebben, who flicked his wrist so quickly it was almost imperceptible. But the general yelped, and moments later his arm went limp around my neck, and he fell back. Kaalek didn't even wait for him to hit the ground before spinning on his heel and slashing at the two soldiers approaching him from behind, their heads whirling into the air.

"Nice throwing," Tara said, putting an arm around Lebben, who looked slightly pale, even with his coppery skin.

I rubbed my neck where the general's arm had squeezed against my flesh. "You're as good a shot as you said you were."

Raas Kaalek strode over to where the general lay, knocked out but not dead. He brought his axe down and buried the blade in the Zagrath's chest. "That's for threatening to execute me."

We all stared down at the dead general for a moment as Kaalek ripped out his axe blade and blood gurgled up out of the Zagrath's chest and soaked his uniform.

"We should get out of here," Tara said, tugging Kaalek by the arm. "We still need to find Raas Vassim."

The sound of a ship entering the atmosphere made us all look up, but it was still not light enough to see what type of ship was descending to the planet's surface. We watched as it dipped below the tree line and disappeared in the distance.

"The village," Lebben said, his voice trembling. "That ship landed near my village!"

CHAPTER THIRTY-FIVE

Juliette

My side ached as we ran through the woods, Lebben taking the lead because he knew the way back to the village by heart. Even though he was shorter than the rest of us—and especially Raas Kaalek—his pace was swift as we tore through the thick underbrush and vines trailing down from the trees. He hadn't spoken since we'd seen the ship descend, but his worry was palpable.

Who had landed in his village? I hoped it was one of the Vandar ships that had slipped through the battle blockade, but I feared it was an imperial ship filled with more helmeted soldiers with blasters. My stomach lurched at the thought of the Carlogians waiting for us in the village.

I couldn't see much as I ran behind Kaalek and Tara, but I didn't mind bringing up the rear. I'd never run so much or so fast, and I tried not to gasp for breath and draw the attention of the others. I pressed a hand to the sharp pain in my side—using my other hand to rub at the itchy flesh on my chest—and pushed myself to keep going.

When Lebben skidded to a stop, followed by Kaalek and Tara, I almost ran into them.

"Not so fast," a voice said, deep and a bit familiar.

"I'm Carlogian," Lebben said through ragged breaths. "I'm not with the empire."

I peered around Kaalek and Tara to see who had stopped us. Light filtered through the leafy canopy above, no longer the silvery glow of moonlight but the warm gold from the rising sun, and I was startled to see Corvak standing in front of Lebben.

"Corvak!" Kaalek said before I could speak. "I heard you were on the planet."

"Raas Kaalek?" Corvak shook his head slightly. "What are you doing here?"

"We promised to always return if the Carlogians needed us," Tara said, stepping closer to the Raas.

Corvak nodded to her. "You are Astrid's sister."

"Tara!" A female with brown skin and dark curls stepped forward, flipping shiny pointed sticks in her hands and hooking them onto her belt. "Danica will be sorry she stayed on the ship and missed you."

"Hey, Tori." Tara pulled the female into a one-armed hug. "I'm not surprised to see you in the middle of another battle."

Tori shrugged one shoulder. "You know me. I never met a fight I didn't like."

More figures emerged from around us, many of them well-muscled males with gold skin, long, dark hair and pointed ears. They wore only leather pants, and had dark tattoos emblazoned on their skin, not to mention ridges running down their bare backs. These must be the bounty hunters who'd fought with Corvak and Raas Vassim on my home world. I'd heard of their appearance, but never seen them. And, of course, my attempt to join their ship had taken an unexpected turn.

"Your ship is on the planet, K'alvek?" Kaalek asked, when a gold-skinned alien with slash marks across his chest muscles stepped forward.

The alien clasped his hand in greeting. "It is hidden well, since we left our pregnant crew mates on it."

Kaalek grinned. "Soon your ship will be filled with the wails of babies."

Tori grunted. "Don't remind me. Pregnant females are bad enough." She jerked her thumb at a young, gold-skinned alien with loose, dark hair. "Not to mention cocky Dothveks."

He smiled at her, his lip curling up as he growled.

"We tracked the Vandar ship that crashed into the water, and the imperial ship that followed it," K'alvek said.

"I was on that ship," I said, both my trembling voice and my jittery scratching at my neck betraying my nerves, but I didn't care. I had no time to exchange pleasantries with the bounty hunters. Now when Vassim was still missing. "So was Raas Vassim. He was taken by the Zagrath but escaped, and we're looking for him."

"Juliette?"

The sound of his gravelly voice made me almost sink to the ground. He pushed through the Dothveks and swept me into his arms, crushing my body to his.

"You're okay," I murmured, burying my head in his neck as he lifted me off the ground. "I thought…" The words died on my lips, my throat too thick with emotion for me to continue.

"I am okay now that I'm holding you," he whispered back, then pulled away and frowned at me. "But you should not have come looking for me. I distracted the Zagrath so you could get away. Not so you could run into danger."

"I guess you've been a bad influence on me, because no way was I going to let you get taken by the empire without a fight."

He pushed my hood back and brushed a curl off my face. "You will make a good Vandar mate, after all."

My face flushed with pleasure at the compliment as he kissed me, my lips melting into his even though I was very aware that we had an audience. When he finally tore his lips from mine and returned me to the ground, I lifted my gaze shyly—right into the face of my sister.

"Sienna?"

She stared at me as if she was looking at a specter. "He said you were here, but I didn't believe him. It was too crazy. You'd never leave home."

"Well, I did," I said, more forcefully than usual. "I ran away to find you. I needed to make amends and my plan was to stow away on the bounty hunter ship and beg you to let me stay."

She cocked an eyebrow at me. "You actually stowed away on a spaceship?"

"The wrong one. That's how I ended up on Raas Vassim's warbird."

Sienna shot him a dark look.

"It wasn't his fault," I said quickly. "And he didn't kidnap me."

She still didn't look convinced, but she looked back at me.

"I'm sorry, Sienna. For everything. I was stupid and selfish and scared of you leaving me. I never should have betrayed you to Donal, or meddled in your life."

She didn't respond, but instead pulled me into a hug, holding me so tightly I could barely breathe. "You're my sister, Juliette. Of course I forgive you."

Relief washed over me as I hugged her back, and I barely noticed the tears as they spilled down my cheeks.

Sienna pulled back and held me by the shoulders. "You're more than welcome to join me on the bounty hunter ship." She glanced back at her new crew mates. "Right, guys?"

"We definitely need more females to offset the Dothvek and Vandar tough-guy energy," Tori said.

Corvak glanced at Raas Vassim but nodded. "My mate's sister is always welcome. You're family."

It was odd to hear tough, gruff Corvak refer to me as family, but it also made my heart swell. It had been a long time since I'd thought of family as anything but a burden or a source of pain.

"Thanks, but I'm actually going to stay with Vassim." I glanced at him, tugging at the neckline of my jumpsuit, the fabric itchy against my hot skin. "If that's okay with him?"

"I do not think you need to ask," Corvak said. "His marks say it all."

I followed Corvak's gaze to the Raas' chest and the dark swirls that were expanding across his shoulders and up his neck as if an invisible hand was inking them as we watched. I lifted a hand to my own chest, and I didn't need to see my skin to know what was happening. My flesh burned, and my mouth went dry.

Raas Vassim touched a hand to his chest then reached over and tugged down my cowl neckline, his eyes widening as he gaped at the exposed flesh of my neck and chest. Then he growled and pulled me to him hard, grabbing my ass and lifting me off the ground. I wrapped my legs around his waist, not caring that everyone was watching as I kissed him.

The world around me disappeared as I sank into Vassim, savoring the softness of his lips as they moved urgently against mine. Only the loud rumbling of more ships made me rip myself away from him and look up.

"More ships, descending to the planet," Raas Kaalek said.

Tara's face was grim. "And it looks like they're all landing in the village."

"Where's Lebben?" I asked, realizing for the first time since we'd stopped that he was no longer with us. Then I knew where he was, and my heart sank. He'd run ahead to his village—alone.

CHAPTER THIRTY-SIX

Vassim

We made no secret of our presence as we ran through the forest toward the village, our footsteps crashing through the brush. Shafts of warm light streamed through the leaves above, burning off the morning mist that clung to the ground. The chirping of night insects had been replaced by bird song, the high notes wafting through the cool air. It would have almost seemed peaceful, if I hadn't known of the battleships and warbirds battling above us.

The Dothveks took the lead as we ran, slashing hanging vines with their curved blades and carving a path for the rest of us. Raas Kaalek and Corvak were close behind them with their mates, who ran fast, considering their shorter legs. I jogged at the back beside Juliette, keeping pace with her slower gait.

"You should run ahead," she said as she heaved in a breath, pausing to lean against a willowy tree. "I'm only slowing you down."

"Do you really think I would be parted from you so quickly?" I stopped with her, touching a finger to the marks swirling across her collarbone. "You are my one true mate, Juliette. I will never leave you."

She smiled up at me. "In the future, I'll leave the battles to you."

"Agreed." I scooped her up in my arms. "For now, I'll carry you."

She didn't protest, winding her arms around my neck. Even though I'd been painfully shocked and then suspended by an energy field, that seemed like a distant memory. My stamina had been restored by the sight of my marks etched across Juliette's skin, and the realization that she was my one true mate. I'd wanted her so desperately that the thought of keeping my promise and returning her to her home had been agonizing. Now, I didn't have to. Not only were we mates, but she'd also chosen to stay with me, even over going with her sister. I held her closer as my legs pumped hard, catching up with the rest of the war party as they burst into the village.

But what I'd expected to see—imperial ships and soldiers in crisp uniforms and shiny helmets—wasn't there. Instead, black Vandar transports sat at either end of the village, their wings stretched out from gaping, round bellies as if ready to take flight. Carlogians milled about with Vandar raiders, Furb scampering around on the ground while Baru chased after him, cursing in Vandar.

"You found him!" Fenrey bustled up to us, his creased face beaming.

I lowered Juliette to the ground. "There are no imperial ships?"

He shook his head. "Lebben asked the same thing and looked just as shocked as you do." The little Carlogian patted my arm. "Your Vandar hordes and resistance fighters took them all out."

Juliette glanced at me and then at Fenrey. "All of them?"

"Isn't it wonderful news?" the Carlogian healer asked, joining us. "No more imperial soldiers on Carlogia Prime. We should have a party to celebrate."

"I love parties," Juliette said. "If only I had time to bake a cake."

I didn't recognize the Vandar raiders milling about with the Carlogian villagers, or the two Raas' striding toward me. Then again, it had been a long time since I'd laid eyes on other hordes, or their warlords.

"Raas Vassim?" The younger Raas addressed me with a click of his heels. "I am Raas Toraan. We are glad to see you out of the hands of the enemy."

"Thank you. I owe a debt of gratitude to Corvak and to the bounty hunters for rescuing me." I nodded to Fenrey and Coxley. "And to the Carlogians for saving my mate."

"Corvak?" the other Raas asked, his brow furrowing in confusion.

"You are Raas Bron," I surmised. I did not say what else was on my tongue, that he was the one who'd exiled the Vandar to Kimithion III. Then again, if Corvak had not been exiled, I never would have responded to his hail for assistance against the Zagrath, and Juliette wouldn't have snuck aboard my ship. In a way, I owed my happiness to the Raas who exiled Corvak.

"I am," he said, squaring his shoulders and clicking his heels.

"Corvak speaks highly of you," I said. "And he has fought bravely."

There was a heavy silence, which Raas Toraan finally filled by clearing his throat. "Between the hordes of Raas Bron, Raas Kaalek, Raas Toraan, and Raas Vassim, along with help from the bounty hunters on the surface and the Valox resistance in the air, all the imperial ships have been destroyed."

"None escaped?" I asked.

Raas Toraan shook his head. "None. Considering how many battleships they sent in hopes of ambushing us, this has done significant damage to the Zagrath fleet, perhaps insurmountable."

"There are some soldiers and a general on the beach," I said. "I left them alive so I could find Juliette."

She slipped her small hand into mine. "They're dead, Vassim."

I gazed down at her. "Don't tell me you killed them?"

She laughed. "No, it was Raas Kaalek and Lebben. He shot a dart at the Zagrath general who'd grabbed me. Once the man was out, Kaalek did the rest."

Anger stirred within me at the thought that the general who'd tormented me had also threatened my mate, but it was quickly replaced by overwhelming relief that the Zagrath was dead. "I will have to thank Lebben and Kaalek."

"All part of the fun," Raas Kaalek said, walking up to us and slapping a hand on Raas Toraan's back. "Right, little brother?"

Raas Toraan groaned and rolled his eyes. "You know I am also a Raas, right Kaalek?"

"But you're still my kid brother." Kaalek threw an arm around Toraan's shoulder. "And I don't get to see you enough."

"I'm busy raiding." Toraan elbowed his brother. "Just like you."

"I thought you might be busy with that pretty little human of yours."

"Mine keeps me just as busy as yours does, Kaalek."

Kaalek blew out a breath. "Then you must be as exhausted as I am." He cut a glance to me. "Don't let their small stature fool you, Vassim, human females are a handful."

I smiled down at Juliette. "I'm looking forward to finding out just how much of a handful myself."

"Tell him, Bron," Kaalek said. "I hear your human mate is as keen for battle as mine is."

Bron shifted on his feet, peering over one shoulder to where a group of human women stood talking—the mates of the other Raas', I assumed. Even though they looked very different from each other, they all looked like they could hold their own against a Raas, dressed in either snug pants and vests or battle kilts like the Vandar.

"I believe I owe your mate an apology."

I turned back to see that Corvak had joined us, his eyes locked on Raas Bron.

The Raas stiffened. "Corvak. I was surprised to discover your presence on the planet."

"Once I helped liberate the planet of Kimithion III from imperial threat, I was offered a position with the bounty hunters. I took it so I could continue to do what I do best—fight against the empire."

"Your battle skill has never been in question," Bron said.

"But my loyalty has." Corvak bent down on one knee. "I never should have challenged your authority. You were only protecting your female. I understand now how that feels."

"You have a mate?" Bron asked.

Corvak nodded but didn't lift his head. "A human."

"My sister," Juliette added.

Bron threw back his head and laughed, the bellowing sound drawing people's attention.

Corvak looked up. "You find this funny, Raas?"

"That you, who scoffed at the idea of human mates, has taken a human female for a mate?" Bron grinned widely at him. "Yes, I find that both fitting and amusing." He motioned for the raider to stand. "Rise, Corvak. Your time in exile has obviously changed you for the better. Who am I to hold a grudge?"

Corvak stood, clicking his heels. "Thank you, Raas."

Bron crossed his arms over his chest. "You are happy flying with the bounty hunters?"

"They are fierce warriors, even the females."

"I hope you aren't too content," I said, stealing a quick glance at Juliette. "I am in need of a battle chief, and I suspect my mate would enjoy having her sister aboard our warbird with her."

"You mean it?" Juliette gasped.

I didn't take my eyes off the Vandar. "If Corvak wishes to fly with my horde, I would be honored to welcome him as my battle chief."

Corvak squared his shoulders. "As much as I regard the Dothveks and their crew, my place is on a Vandar horde. I would be honored to raid with you."

Fenrey dabbed at his eyes. "I love happy endings."

Juliette stood on her tiptoes and whispered in my ear, "Have I told you lately how much I adore you?"

My heart stuttered in my chest. "You have not told me at all."

She tugged my hand, pulling me away from the other warlords and toward the nearest Vandar transport. "Then let me show you."

CHAPTER THIRTY-SEVEN

Juliette

"Why are we going in here?" Vassim asked, as I pulled him onto the empty transport.

"Because everyone is busy celebrating the victory against the empire, and no one would think of looking in here." She pulled me away from the central compartment and opened a narrow door. "Besides, I thought you should see how I stowed away on your ships. Twice."

He eyed the dark storage closet warily. "Neither of those attempts turned out well for you."

"I don't know about that," I told him, tugging him into the small space with me. I closed the door, encasing us in darkness. "My first attempt did lead me to you, so I'd consider that a good thing, wouldn't you?"

"A very good thing."

I ran my hands up his bare chest until I found his shoulders and then tangled my fingers in his hair. I pulled his head down until his lips were on mine. I let myself sink into the kiss, savoring the forbidden thrill of kissing the Raas when everyone else was gathered outside. It was so far from what I'd normally do that the excitement made my heart race. Being with the Raas had definitely awakened a side of me I didn't know I had—a side I couldn't wait to explore more fully as the mate of a Vandar.

When I tore my lips from his, we were both panting.

"Wait," I said. "If we both have mating marks, then that means the curse is broken, right?"

"I don't know." He hesitated. "And I don't care."

"What do you mean, you don't care?" Even though I was secretly pleased to hear that he wasn't obsessed with the curse anymore, I was still shocked. "That was the entire reason you dragged me to that creepy, mystical planet and made a deal to keep me on your ship."

His breath was warm on my neck as he held me. "That was before I knew you were mine. It doesn't matter if the curse is broken or not. If I have you, nothing else is important. *Tvek* the curse."

A laugh bubbled up in my throat. "Okay then, *tvek* the curse."

He chuckled low and deep, the resonance of his voice sending a shiver down my spine. "I'll get you talking like a Vandar, after all."

"You're not afraid I'm too fragile to be a Raas' mate?" I asked, almost afraid to hear the answer.

"You've shown that you have the heart of a warrior when you came to rescue me. That is all that's needed to be a mate to a

Vandar." He moved his hands down to my ass and squeezed. "Besides, I don't want you to be too tough. I like your soft curves."

I groaned in mock horror. "Then you're in luck, because I've got plenty of them."

"And I love all of them."

My breath caught in my throat. He'd never said the word before, and I'd honestly never imagined that someone as fierce and battle-hardened as him would. "You do?"

"I love everything about you, Juliette."

I stifled a sob. No one had ever told me they loved me. Not like that. I yanked him to me, needing to feel his body on mine, needing to feel him *in* me. As I kissed him wildly, I tugged at the sleeves of my jumpsuit, cursing the one-piece outfit. It had been so perfect for a mission in the woods, but it was not ideal for a romp in a closet.

Vassim helped me, pulling the fabric over my shoulders and my waist, moaning as my breasts spilled out of the tight confines. When we'd managed to work the jumpsuit over my hips, he spun me around as I shimmied the fabric the rest of the way to my feet.

"Juliette," he husked, reaching around and palming my breasts in his large hands as I bent over.

"I want to feel you inside me, Raas." My thighs were already slick with desire, and I let out a breathy sigh when he dragged his cock between them and notched it at my opening.

"Your wish is my command, mate." Then he plunged himself into me with a single, deep thrust.

I gasped at the sudden stretch, but the pleasure that accompanied it made me moan and rock back into him. "More, Vassim. I want more."

He quickly obliged, pounding into me again and again as he slipped his tail up between my legs while he thumbed my nipples. The delicious sensation of being filled by him was soon joined by the tip of his tail circling my swollen nub. I arched back as he worked his tail between my legs and his cock inside me, the illicit thrill making me writhe wildly. He slid one hand from my breast to my hair, fisting it and pulling it back so my neck was exposed and then biting down on my bare flesh.

"You are mine," he growled, the noise primal and rough as it vibrated along the surface of my skin.

I bucked against him as my body quivered and then shattered, clenching his cock over and over. He slid his hand up to circle my neck and then to my mouth, where I bit down on the finger he put between my lips. Vassim reared back and buried his cock deep, letting out a roar I was sure rattled the hull and could be heard outside the ship.

"See?" I said between uneven breaths. "I knew you'd like my closet."

"It's not your closet I like so much." He pulled his cock out and then the furry tip of his tail was pushing inside me. "It's you, Juliette. I can't get enough of your perfect body."

I whimpered as he dragged his tail in and out of me slowly. "You have me—all of me."

"That's all I've ever truly desired." He tilted my head back and crushed his mouth to mine in a deep claiming kiss that didn't end until I'd come again with his tail inside me.

I sighed when I realized that being truly adored was all I'd ever wanted as well—and I'd found it in the most unexpected place and with someone I'd once believed was irredeemable.

Turning around, I tugged my jumpsuit back up. "Now I'm going to take you to bed."

He made a hungry noise in the back of his throat, and I laughed, knowing that he was going to be surprised when I tucked him into bed for a long sleep he so badly needed.

CHAPTER THIRTY-EIGHT

Vassim

"I don't understand." I stared at the small bedroom carved into the tunnel. The dirt roof was arched above a wooden bed covered with a quilt and a pair of fluffy pillows. The air smelled slightly of the loamy earth and the tallow of burning candles lit on the bedside tables.

"I know it isn't much," Fenrey said, fluttering a hand and finally pressing it to his paisley ascot. "We built it during the Zagrath occupation. In case my son came home, and I needed to hide him." His voice broke, and he waved his hands away. "But Lebben came home safely, and I've rarely had use for this room." He chuckled. "At least after Tara and Kaalek left."

"Thank you," Juliette said. "It's perfect. He won't stay long."

"He?" I swung my head to her as she prodded me toward the bed. "I thought…" I glanced at the little Carlogian. I didn't want to say what I'd thought in front of the alien, but his cheeks colored nonetheless.

"I'll leave you two," he stammered, backing from the arched doorway and into the tunnel illuminated by string lights.

Juliette gave me a hard shove, and I fell backward onto the bed, bouncing slightly on the soft mattress. I reached out to grab her but she danced away.

She folded back the neckline of her jumpsuit to reveal the black swirls etched into her skin. "These marks mean we're true mates, right?"

I brushed my fingers over my throat where the expanding marks were still hot to the touch. "They do."

"Then that means the curse should be broken, and you should be able to sleep without being tortured by the memories of that battle."

I looked back at the bed and loosed a breath. It was almost too much to think the curse might finally have relinquished its hold on me. "But what if…?"

She stepped closer and fell forward, pushing me the rest of the way down until we were both lying flat on the bed. "Only one way to find out, Raas."

I growled as I felt her soft curves pressed into me, but she put her fingertips over my eyelids and closed them. "I'll be right here when you wake up." She then feathered kisses across my lids. "Always."

I wanted to tell her I wasn't tired and flip her onto her back, but a wave of exhaustion and contentment flooded my body, making me too lethargic to move.

"Always," I murmured as I drifted into the first deep, peaceful sleep I'd had in longer than I could remember, my thoughts filled with Juliette. "Forever."

EPILOGUE

"It's about time," Sienna said, standing inside her quarters and waving me in.

I stepped inside and swept a gaze across the room that held a large bed and a sitting area, as well as a round table for dining. Although there was only one Raas suite on the warbird, Raas Vassim had insisted on knocking out some walls and combining several regular officer quarters—freed up by raiders who wished to hang up their battle axes—into a larger space for Corvak and my sister to share. The design was decidedly Vandar, with the furniture glossy black and bolted to the floor for safely, but the pops of colorful cushions were all Sienna.

"Corvak isn't here?" I asked, peering toward the bathroom, which, while it wasn't as spacious as the bathing chamber I shared with Vassim, still had an open, black-stone shower. Since the Vandar were so casual about nudity, the last thing I wanted was to surprise a naked Corvak as he strode from the shower. I might be a mate to a Vandar, but Corvak still made me nervous.

Maybe it was because I'd been intimidated of him when he'd been on Kimithion III, or maybe it was because he could still be pretty intense when talking about battle plans, but my sister's mate still made me jumpy.

"He's on the command deck," Sienna said. "He and your guy are planning their next meet-up with Raas Bron's horde on Galatia I."

"Another planet that overthrew the empire?"

Sienna nodded, with a satisfied grin. "Who knew that when all the hordes took out that fleet at Carlogia Prime, the empire would start to lose its hold on the galaxy?"

"I guess it's a good thing, but I never anticipated we'd be so busy assisting planets who'd liberated themselves from the Zagrath."

"It's not the same as raiding, and I know Corvak misses actual battles, but this is what the Vandar have always worked for—a galaxy free from imperial control." She reached for the container in my hands. "Now, did you bring them or what?"

I swatted playfully at her hand. "Always so greedy. I guess some things haven't changed."

She groaned and followed me to the table where I set down the box and opened it to reveal a batch of freshly baked rolls dusted with sugar. "Pace yourself. You know I'm running low on sugar."

Sienna took a warm roll and bit into it, her eyes fluttering closed briefly as she moaned. "One thing about Vandar culture I'll never get—their lack of love for sugar."

"That may be changing. There seems to be serious demand for these on board." I sat down and plucked a roll from the box, even though I didn't have much of an appetite for the sweet treats after spending so long baking them. Luckily, I'd been teaching Baru to bake alongside me, so he could step in when I was all "baked out." "Vassim promised to get more sugar for me at our next supply stop."

My sister gave me a wicked grin. "I'll bet he did. What else has the Raas promised you since you officially became his Raisa, and he started walking around the ship humming to himself like a lovesick Gerwyn?"

"He does not sound anything like Furb." I shot her a look, even though my lips twitched up at the comparison to my purring pet.

She smirked at me. "Whatever you say. All I know is what Corvak tells me. The crew no longer worries about running into a deranged Raas wandering the halls. Now, he's too busy in his quarters with his new mate to stalk around in the shadows of the ship."

"He was never deranged." My defenses went up on behalf of my mate, even though Sienna was only speaking the truth.

"I know, I know." She waved a hand in the air. "It was that weird curse that you broke. All I'm saying is that it's a good thing. The crew is happier, the Raas is happier, and you are definitely happier than I've ever seen you." She tilted her head at me. "You're almost glowing."

My cheeks warmed. "I'm not the only one. You light up when Corvak's around, and he gets a ridiculous grin on his face."

"What can I say? I'm a sucker for a hot guy in a skirt?"

I shook my head at her, laughing. Despite our playful teasing, it was true that life on the Vandar warbird and with our respective mates was good. Raas Vassim's curse had vanished on Carlogia Prime, and he'd slept for so long I'd feared he might never wake up. But he did, and with an appetite for me that had kept us in

Fenrey's secret tunnel room for such an extended period of time that I was afraid we'd miss the transport back to the horde ship.

Corvak had taken to his new position as battle chief in Raas Vassim's horde as if he'd been born into it, bonding with the *majak*, Taan, and developing lengthy plans for taking out the last remaining Zagrath strongholds. Luckily, the other hordes had remained to aid in crushing any last Zagrath outposts, so our horde had been assisted over the past two standard lunar cycles by Raas Bron, Raas Kaalek, and Raas Toraan.

"You don't regret leaving the bounty hunter ship?" I asked.

Sienna brushed some sugar crystals off her lips. "I'm not going to lie. The female bounty hunters were badass bitches, and I miss being on the front lines of the battles. The Vandar still aren't keen on having me fight with them."

"I doubt the horde's battle chief wants to worry about his mate when he sends raiders into battle."

My sister frowned. "At least he's letting me go down to the planets they liberate and help train the people to defend themselves. That's kept me busy. But Corvak is so much happier being back on a Vandar horde that I'm fine with fighting less." She winked at me. "He does still spar with me in the battle ring, so I won't get rusty."

I blushed, realizing I hadn't been aware that my sister was doing any of this. I'd been spending so much time in bed—and in the baths and on the floor and up against the walls—with Vassim that I hadn't had much time to check on Sienna. Hence the peace offering with sweet bread.

"What about you, little sister?" Sienna eyed me. "I never would have thought you'd take to being a Vandar mate so seamlessly, and with a Raas no less. You're sure he hasn't brainwashed you?"

"I'm sure."

"Well, like I said, life on a horde agrees with you." She gave me a quick one-over. "And is it possible that your boobs have gotten bigger?"

"Look who's talking," I teased her, pointing to the swell of her breasts peeking above the scoop neck of her black shirt. "Yours definitely are. Maybe it's something in the Vandar water."

She peeked at her own cleavage and then back at mine. "*Tvekking* hell."

"What? Since when do you use Vandar curses?"

"They're even better than old Earth curses," she said, glancing suspiciously at the box of breads. "Why aren't you eating any of your baking?"

"My stomach has been acting weird. It's no biggie," I said, using one of her favorite Earth phrases.

"Not yet it isn't," Sienna muttered, scraping a hand through her loose hair with a laugh.

"What are you talking about?"

"Come on, Juliette. I know you aren't this naïve anymore. Nausea, bigger boobs? We're both pregnant."

I stared at her, cataloging all the mornings I'd woken up feeling queasy, and how tender my breasts had become. "*Tvek*, you're right."

"See? Sometimes only a Vandar curse will do."

Despite my shock, I placed a hand over my mouth as uncontrollable laughter bubbled up in my throat. "What are Vassim and Corvak going to say?"

"About what?" Corvak asked, the door to the quarters sliding open to reveal both Vandar raiders.

"Baru told me you were visiting your sister," Vassim said, following his battle chief inside. "He also said you baked."

I stared at him, unable to think of a single response.

"Is everything okay?" Corvak finally asked, looking from me to Sienna.

Sienna walked over to her mate and pressed her hands to his bare chest. "Do you remember how Tori was complaining about the babies they were going to have on board the ship soon?"

He nodded. "She said she was going to move into one of the escape pods when the three babies arrived."

"What would say to two babies on this ship?"

Corvak looked down at her, his face blank for a moment. Then his eyes widened. "You're having two babies?"

"No." She slapped his chest. "Juliette is having one, and I'm having one. At least, we're pretty sure we are. We'll have to confirm it."

Raas Vassim crossed to me in two long strides, putting a hand to my belly. "Is this true?"

I nodded as the backs of my eyelids pricked with happy tears. "I think so."

He dropped to his knees, placing a kiss on my belly and murmuring something in Vandar. Then he stood and pulled me into an embrace, lifting me off my toes.

"I take it you're happy?" I asked, seeing Corvak hugging my sister behind us.

"I didn't think I could be happier than I already was with you," Vassim whispered. "But now I am. We're going to be a family."

"A big family," Sienna said, holding out her hand for me to take.

I grabbed her hand with one of mine and took Vassim's hand in the other, squeezing them both. I finally had the family I'd always dreamed about—and it was only the beginning.

———

Thank you for reading PROVOKED! If you liked this alien barbarian romance, you'll love Tana Stone's *Barbarians of the Sand Planet* series (featuring the bounty hunters and hot Dothveks you met in this book).

As captain of the galaxy's only all-female bounty hunter crew, Danica thought she was prepared for anything. Until they crashed on a primitive desert planet, and she was separated from her crew. She wasn't expecting to be saved by a gorgeous, gold-skinned alien barbarian who could read her mind—and make her heart race.

One click BOUNTY now>

> "Omg love! Great kicka$$ ladies, and swoonworthy mancandy. "- Amazon Reviewer

———

This book has been edited and proofed, but typos are like little gremlins that like to sneak in when we're not looking. If you spot a typo, please report it to: tana@tanastone.com
Thank you!!

ALSO BY TANA STONE

Raider Warlords of the Vandar Series:

POSSESSED (also available in AUDIO)

PLUNDERED (also available in AUDIO)

PILLAGED (also available in AUDIO)

PURSUED

PUNISHED

PROVOKED

Alien Academy Series:

ROGUE (also available in AUDIO)

The Tribute Brides of the Drexian Warriors Series:

TAMED (also available in AUDIO)

SEIZED (also available in AUDIO)

EXPOSED (also available in AUDIO)

RANSOMED (also available in AUDIO)

FORBIDDEN (also available in AUDIO)

BOUND (also available in AUDIO)

JINGLED (A Holiday Novella)

CRAVED (also available in AUDIO)

STOLEN

SCARRED

The Barbarians of the Sand Planet Series:

BOUNTY (also available in AUDIO)

CAPTIVE (also available in AUDIO)

TORMENT (also available on AUDIO)

TRIBUTE (also available as AUDIO)

SAVAGE

CLAIM

TANA STONE books available as audiobooks!

RAIDER WARLORDS OF THE VANDAR:

POSSESSED on AUDIBLE

PLUNDERED on AUDIBLE

PILLAGED on AUDIBLE

Alien Academy Series:

ROGUE on AUDIBLE

BARBARIANS OF THE SAND PLANET

BOUNTY on AUDIBLE

CAPTIVE on AUDIBLE

TORMENT on AUDIBLE

TRIBUTE on AUDIBLE

TRIBUTE BRIDES OF THE DREXIAN WARRIORS

TAMED on AUDIBLE

SEIZED on AUDIBLE

EXPOSED on AUDIBLE

RANSOMED on AUDIBLE

FORBIDDEN on AUDIBLE

BOUND on AUDIBLE

CRAVED on AUDIBLE

ABOUT THE AUTHOR

Tana Stone is a bestselling sci-fi romance author who loves sexy aliens and independent heroines. Her favorite superhero is Thor (with Aquaman a close second because, well, Jason Momoa), her favorite dessert is key lime pie (okay, fine, *all* pie), and she loves Star Wars and Star Trek equally. She still laments the loss of *Firefly*.

She has one husband, two teenagers, and two neurotic cats. She sometimes wishes she could teleport to a holographic space station like the one in her tribute brides series (or maybe vacation at the oasis with the sand planet barbarians). :-)

She loves hearing from readers! Email her any questions or comments at tana@tanastone.com.

Want to hang out with Tana in her private Facebook group? Join on all the fun at: https://www.facebook.com/groups/tanastonestributes/

Copyright © 2021 by Broadmoor Books

Cover Design by Croco Designs

Editing by Tanya Saari

All rights reserved.

No part of this book may be reproduced in any form or by any electronic or mechanical means, including information storage and retrieval systems, without written permission from the author, except for the use of brief quotations in a book review.

This is a work of fiction. Names, characters, places, and incidents are the products of the author's imagination or are used fictitiously and are not to be construed as real. Any resemblance to actual events, locales, organizations, or persons, living or dead, is entirely coincidental.

Printed in Great Britain
by Amazon